U0025373

俗辣
英文俚語
特搜

Modern English Slang for You

作　者・**LiLi Amanda Crum**

審訂者・**Helen Yeh**

譯　者・**羅慕謙**

通常英語學習者在教室裡學的單字、文法都是中規中矩、生硬刻板的正式用法，但其實英語人士說的英文是很活的，就像中文常說「很瞎」、「有梗」、「傻眼」一樣，英語人士在日常對話、非正式的社交場合中也會大量使用這類俚語，結果只學正式用法的學習者一聽到英語俚語時，就算單字很簡單，也不懂對方的意思。為了能看懂英美影劇、與英語人士互動流暢，英語學習者應多學更道地的俗諺俚語，掌握英語文化的精髓。

俚語是出現在日常生活中非正式，且較口語的用語，往往只流行幾年，不斷地汰舊換新，它可能是新詞，也可能是外來語，也可能是特定群體常用的專門用語，例如黑人、衝浪迷、大學生等，有些俚語更涉及禁忌話題，像是髒話、吸毒、性交等。俚語被用來傳達說話者的語氣、態度，通常給人的感覺是通俗、幽默、輕鬆，有時甚至是辛辣。

本書特意蒐羅美國、加拿大、英國、澳洲等地最常用的俚語，按字母排序，共近600個詞條，每個單元以核心單字為主，羅列不同詞義，收錄相關片語，並針對不同詞義撰寫實用例句，描繪使用情境，搭配精采插圖及MP3朗讀，讓讀者能完全掌握語調、意義及使用時機。

由於俚語多用於非正式場合，所以使用時一定要注意場合和時機，故本書補充了俚語用法、起源、使用地區、族群、禁忌等相關學習內容，透過理解語言背後的文化意涵，加深印象，讓你能正確掌握俚語的用法，不須死背硬記。

本書適合凡欲與英語人士交流者，年齡層為大學、研究所及社會人士，亦可作為翻譯人士、英語教師之進修工具。讀者可將此書當作教科書來精讀，也可以當作參考書來查詢陌生的俚語。

LiLi Amanda Crum

User Guide

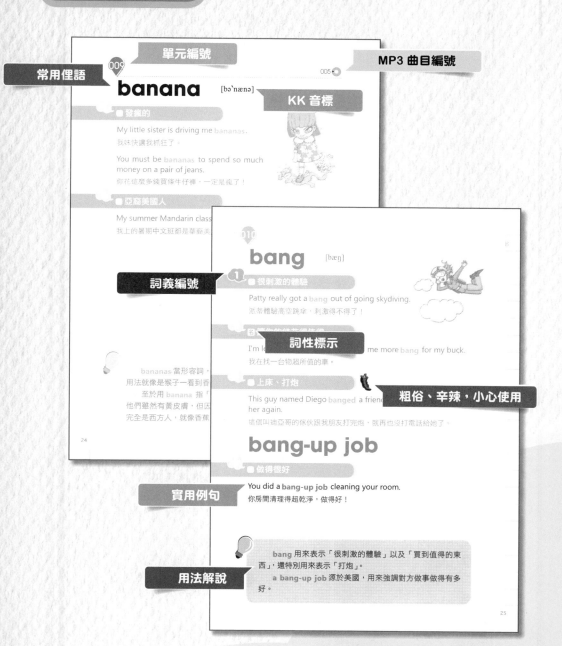

單元編號

MP3 曲目編號

常用俚語

009

banana [bəˋnænə]

KK 音標

005

● 發瘋的

My little sister is driving me bananas.
我妹快讓我抓狂了。

You must be bananas to spend so much money on a pair of jeans.
你花這麼多錢買條牛仔褲，一定是瘋了！

● 亞裔美國人

My summer Mandarin class
我上的暑期中文班都是華裔美

bananas 當形容詞，
用法就像是猴子一看到香
至於用 banana 指「
他們雖然有黃皮膚，但因
完全是西方人，就像香蕉

24

詞義編號

010

bang [bæŋ]

1 ● 很刺激的體驗

Patty really got a bang out of going skydiving.
派蒂體驗高空跳傘，刺激得不得了！

詞性標示

me more bang for my buck.
我在找一台物超所值的車。

● 上床、打炮

粗俗、辛辣，小心使用

This guy named Diego banged a friend
her again.
這個叫迪亞哥的傢伙跟我朋友打完炮，就再也沒打電話給她了。

bang-up job

● 做得很好

實用例句

You did a bang-up job cleaning your room.
你房間清理得超乾淨，做得好！

用法解說

bang 用來表示「很刺激的體驗」以及「買到值得的東西」，還特別用來表示「打炮」。
a bang-up job 源於美國，用來強調對方做事做得有多好。

25

contents

contents

A

001

ace [es]

1 名 優秀、傑出的人

Amanda is an **ace** at math.

阿曼達是數學達人。

2 動 某人某件事表現優異

Nora **aced** her Chinese oral exam.

諾拉中文口試考得超棒。

　　ace 原意指網球或高爾夫球比賽中的得分，同時也是撲克牌中的「A」。

　　ace 的原意都具有正面意義，它當俚語時，也是如此。它可指「某方面很強的達人」，也可指「某人在某件事上表現優異」。

　　這個字目前依然廣泛用於日常生活的各種場合中，像是在校考試成績很好，或是工作、休閒活動表現優異的時候。

ain't [ent]

1 am not 的縮寫

You don't have to say it to me twice. I **ain't** stupid.
你不用把話説兩遍，我沒那麼笨！

2 is not 的縮寫

It **ain't** that bad!
沒那麼糟啦！

3 are not 的縮寫

We **ain't** the only ones with problems finding a job.
不是只有我們找工作碰壁。

You **ain't** finished with that, are you?
你沒弄完，對吧？

4 have not 的縮寫

I **ain't** spoken to him yet, but I will.
我還沒跟他説到話，但我遲早會的。

　　ain't 是 am not、is not、are not 或 have not 的縮寫，一般認為是不正式的英文，所以在學校、工作或專業場合與人交談時，最好不要用 ain't。在正式的書面英文中，也要避免使用。不過，現在有越來越多新聞在口語和書面英文中使用 ain't，目的是為了加強語氣，並展現出口語化的風格。

airhead [ˈɛrˌhɛd]

1 名 笨蛋

Luke is such an **airhead**. He doesn't even know how to spell basic words.

路克很笨，連拼基本單字都不會。

2 名 心不在焉、沒頭沒腦的人

Tracy and Naomi can be such **airheads**. They always forget to take their keys with them when they leave the apartment.

崔西和娜歐蜜真是恍神，每次出門都忘了帶鑰匙。

3 名 腦袋裡除了空氣，什麼都沒有

The waitress at the restaurant was a total **airhead**. It took her three times to get the order right!

那個餐廳女服務生的腦袋有洞，她問了三次才搞清楚我們要點什麼。

 airhead 多當俚語使用，本義「空軍前進基地」反而很少用。顧名思義，一個人的腦袋充滿了空氣，想當然他不會太聰明，所以現在多用 airhead 來指沒腦袋、少根筋的人。

amped [æmpt]

1 形 興奮的、熱切渴望的、迫不及待的

The surfers are really **amped** up to ride the huge waves brought in by the storm last night.

昨夜暴風雨帶來了超讚的浪，衝浪迷很興奮可以衝個過癮。

Jen is **amped** that she will be leaving for Italy in five days.

珍迫不及待，再五天她就要去義大利了。

2 形 生氣或難過

Noreen's parents got her so **amped** because they said she couldn't see her boyfriend Matt anymore.

諾琳被爸媽氣死了，因為他們不准她再見她男友麥特了。

　　當俚語時 **amped** 是形容詞，來源有兩種說法，一是來自 amplify，藉由增加內容擴充物體的體積，另一個是跟安非他命（amphetamine）有關，因為吸毒以後很嗨，所以當我們說一個人很 amped，就表示他很興奮、很嗨，像是體內注入了無限的能量。

003

ass [æs]

1 名 笨蛋、白痴

Matthew made a total **ass** of himself when he spilled his drink on the girl on the dance floor.

那天在舞池裡麥修把飲料灑在那女的身上,真是豬頭。

2 名 人或身體

Get your **ass** over here! I want to talk to you.

快給我滾過來,我有話要跟你說。

3 字尾 極度的、非常的

Albert went deep sea fishing yesterday and he caught a big-**ass** fish!

艾柏特昨天出海釣魚,釣到一條超大的魚!

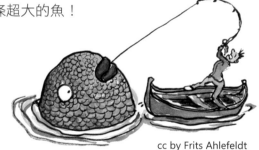

cc by Frits Ahlefeldt

ass除了「屁股」和「驢子」這兩個本義,還有許多互不相干的俚語用法;它可以罵人「白痴」,指「人」,以及當字尾,強調「非常的」,通常帶有貶義,如fat-ass(超肥的)。

多數人認為ass很粗俗,但還是ass不離口。ass是個使用已久,而且一生都會用到的字。

006

awesome [ˈɔsəm]

1 形 很酷的、很棒的

I met an **awesome** girl the other day. Her name is Sophia.
我前幾天認識一個很優的美眉,她叫蘇菲亞。

2 嘆 表示同意

"Wanna go surfing?"
"**Awesome**, dude!"
「要不要去衝浪?」
「好啊!」

3 形 很讚的事情或東西

I just saw the most **awesome** action movie, *Lucy*. Have you seen it?
我剛看了有史以來最棒的動作電影《露西》,你看過沒?

awesome 源自美國西岸的衝浪圈,像是:

That was one awesome ride!
剛剛的浪衝起來真過癮!

現在 awesome 已經廣為流傳,它原是形容詞,用來表示「令人敬畏的」或是「體積龐大」;當俚語用時,也是形容詞,用來表示「某事物真的很酷、很讚」,或是當感嘆語表示「同意」。

004 ▶

bag [bæg]

1 🔊 逮捕

The robber almost got away but the police **bagged** him.

那個搶匪差點就逃走了，不過警方還是逮到他了。

2 🔊 隱藏

Jessie wanted to bring food into the movie theater so she had to **bag** it.

潔西想帶食物進電影院，所以她得把東西藏在袋子裡。

3 🔊 停止或中斷

The New York Mets are down by 5 runs; let's **bag** this game and go get a bite to eat!

紐約大都會隊已經讓對手打出五支全壘打了，我看不下去了，去吃東西吧！

4 🔊 在別人拿到前，先取得某物

We managed to **bag** the best seats in the house even though we got our tickets at the last minute.

雖然我們最後一刻才買（拿）到票，居然還搶到劇院最好的座位。

5 🔊 討厭的女人

Look at that old **bag**. She's got to be the meanest neighbor ever!

看看那個老查某，她一定是世上最爛的鄰居。

6 名 一包毒品

The man bought a **bag** of marijuana from the man standing on the street corner.

那男人跟街角那個男的買了一包大麻。

in the bag

7 慣 喝醉

After a night of drinking, Lydia was **in the bag**.

喝了一夜，莉蒂亞喝醉了。

8 慣 明確的；篤定的

The pitcher knew he had it **in the bag**; he was going to finish the game with a shutout.

投手穩操勝券，他要讓對方一分也得不到，來結束這場比賽。

bag 原來是「袋子」的意思，與「裝袋」的動作有點關聯，大部分俚語用法都源於美國，「批評」的用法則出現於澳洲及紐西蘭。

bag 當動詞時，可指「逮捕」、「藏起來」或「中斷」，多用於表達負面意義；當名詞時，可指「讓人討厭的女人」。

另外，販賣毒品或使用毒品的人會用它來表示「毒品」。千萬要仔細區分用法，用錯了可是會很糗的。

一切猶如探囊取物，你想做到的每件事都可以 in the bag，這表示「你握有勝算」，不過，如果你在美國以外説 in the bag，對方可能會把某件東西裝進袋子交給你。

ball [bɔl]

1 名 狂歡

A group of us went out dancing the other night. We had a **ball**!

前幾天晚上我們去跳舞，玩得可瘋了！

2 名 睪丸

I can't stand it when guys scratch their **balls** in public.

我受不了男生在公眾場合搔他們蛋蛋的癢。

3 動 上床

Did you hear about Michael? He **balled** that girl he met at the bar last night.

你聽說麥可做了什麼嗎？他跟昨晚在酒吧認識的那個女生上床了。

4 名 勇氣、膽量

David finally got the **balls** to ask Ruth out on a date.

大衛終於有種邀茹絲去約會了。

5 名 胡說、廢話

What is he talking about? That's a bunch of **balls**. I never said that!

他在說什麼啊？黑白講！我根本沒說過那種話！

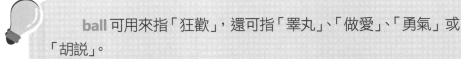

　　ball 可用來指「狂歡」，還可指「睪丸」、「做愛」、「勇氣」或「胡說」。

　　It takes balls to do something 也很常用，意「有種去做什麼事」。如：

It takes a lot of balls to stand up for what you think is right.
要捍衛你認為對的事，需要很大的勇氣。

009

banana [bəˈnænə]

1 形 發瘋的

My little sister is driving me **bananas**.
我妹快讓我抓狂了。

You must be **bananas** to spend so much money on a pair of jeans.
你花這麼多錢買條牛仔褲，一定是瘋了！

2 名 亞裔美國人

My summer Mandarin class is filled with **bananas**.
我上的暑期中文班都是華裔美人。

　　bananas 當形容詞，一定要加 s，表示「發瘋的」，這個用法就像是猴子一看到香蕉就發狂一樣！

　　至於用 **banana** 指「亞裔美國人」，大部分是指中國人，他們雖然有黃皮膚，但因為從小生長在北美地區，行事作風完全是西方人，就像香蕉皮是黃的，香蕉肉是白的一樣。

010

bang [bæŋ]

1 名 很刺激的體驗

Patty really got a **bang** out of going skydiving.
派蒂體驗高空跳傘，刺激得不得了！

2 名 讓你的錢花得值得

I'm looking for a car that will give me more **bang** for my buck.
我在找一台物超所值的車。

3 動 上床、打炮

This guy named Diego **banged** a friend of mine and never called her again.
這個叫迪亞哥的傢伙跟我朋友打完炮，就再也沒打電話給她了。

bang-up job

4 慣 做得很好

You did a **bang-up job** cleaning your room.
你房間清理得超乾淨，做得好！

　　bang 用來表示「很刺激的體驗」以及「買到值得的東西」，還特別用來表示「打炮」。
　　a bang-up job 源於美國，用來強調對方做事做得有多好。

beast   [bist]

1  名 性犯罪者、性侵幼童者

The **beast** went to prison for the horrific crimes he committed against minors.

這畜生對幼童犯下可怕的罪行，被判入獄。

2 名 某方面很強的人

Matt is a **beast** at football.

麥特是橄欖球猛將。

3 名 看起來肌肉大塊到令人害怕的人

That boxer is a **beast**.

那拳擊手是頭猛獸。

美國的性犯罪者常被稱為 **beast**，英國人也如此稱性侵幼童者。

此外，beast 也可以指某方面很強的人，以及那些肌肉超大、看起來有點可怕的猛男。

012

beef [bif]

1 名 抱怨

I told my roommate that I had a **beef** with her. She shouldn't have taken my shirt without asking.

我跟我室友說，她太超過了，竟然不問一聲就把我的襯衫拿去穿。

2 動 抱怨

Jack was **beefing** about how badly the company was being run.

傑克在抱怨公司經營得很差。

3 名 爭執

The two drunks at the bar had a **beef** with each other over who had won the game.

酒吧裡兩個醉鬼在爭到底誰贏了比賽。

　　beef原意是「牛肉」，當俚語時，用來表示「抱怨」或「爭論」。諷刺的是，如果牛知道自己會被拿來當成這樣的俚語，一定會 have a beef with the farmer（和農場主人吵架），絕不會成為 beef for the farmer（農場主人的牛肉）了。

013

bent [bɛnt]

1 形 不正直的、墮落的

The police department in this area is filled with **bent** cops.
這區的警察都很黑。

2 形 偷來的（商品、貨物）

The warehouse was full of **bent** items.
倉庫堆滿了贓物。

3 形 發狂、生氣的

Simon got all **bent** out of shape because we were late for his party.
賽門氣炸了，因為我們去參加他的派對時都遲到了。

bent on

4 慣 決心要做某事

Albert was **bent on** doing everything his own way.
艾柏特決心做每件事都要照他的方式來。

bent 原來表示「東西彎了」，或是「改變形狀了」，它的俚語用法跟原意相當接近，可指「墮落的」、「生氣的」，若是發生了這些情況，表示這個人已經脫離原來的軌道。

而 **bent on** 表示人下決心，要做什麼事，通常都是以 bend 的過去分詞出現，有「傾向於」的意思。

bitch [bɪtʃ]

1 名 壞心或討人厭的女人

The other day some woman crashed into my friend's car and acted like a complete **bitch** about the whole thing.

前幾天有個女的突然撞我朋友的車,像個潑婦一樣。

2 名 煩人或累人的工作

It's a **bitch** to have to work on weekends.

煩死了,週末還得工作!

3 名 女朋友

I find it offensive when a guy refers to his girlfriend as his "**bitch**."

我覺得男生把女朋友叫作「馬子」,很不尊重人。

bitchin'

4 動 說某人的不是、抱怨

Kathy is constantly **bitchin'** about her coworkers.

凱西老是在靠北她同事。

5 形 令人印象深刻的

That party was **bitchin'**. No one wanted to go home towards the end.

這個趴超讚的,到最後沒人想回家。

bitchy

形 挖苦的、惡意的

I've noticed that people who are **bitchy** rarely have any close friends.

我注意到愛酸人的人幾乎沒有密友。

bitch 原指「母狗」，當俚語時可指「壞心的人」或「討厭的女生」，也可指「抱怨某人的言行」或是「發牢騷」。**bitch**、**bitchin'**、**bitchy** 是最常見的俚語用法，已經廣為流傳，被叫 bitch 或是被人勸告 stop bitchin' 都不是很光采的事。

不過，有些情況下 **bitchin'** 可用來描述「絕佳」、「超讚」的事，像是遇到衝浪者夢寐以求的大浪時會說：

Now that was a bitchin' wave. It was extremely impressive!

那可是超棒的浪，超讚的！

008

blast [blæst]

1 名 愉快的經驗

Amanda and Mary had a **blast** when they went to California.

亞曼達和瑪莉去加州玩得超開心。

blasted

2 形 爛醉如泥

Jennie was so **blasted** the other night that she lost her purse on her way home.

珍妮那天晚上喝得爛醉，結果回家路上把錢包搞丟了。

3 動 嚴厲批評

The media **blasted** the president's foreign policy.

媒體痛批總統的外交政策。

 blast原指「起飛」或「爆炸」。如果你和朋友出去玩、開派對，或是玩得非常開心，你就可以說I'm having a blast.。

016

blow [blo]

1 動 亂花錢

Whenever Peter gets any money he **blows** it on CDs and concert tickets.

彼得每次一有錢，就砸錢買 CD 和演唱會門票。

2 名 古柯鹼

You'd be surprised at how many famous people do **blow**.

你可能會很驚訝很多名人吸古柯鹼。

3 名 吸一口毒品

Take a **blow** and pass it on, man!

老兄，哈一口，傳下去吧！

4 動 離開

Let's **blow** this place; we've been here for hours.

我們離開這裡吧，已經待了好幾個鐘頭了。

5 動 輸錢

John **blew** all his savings on horse racing.

約翰賭馬輸光所有積蓄。

blow chunks

6 動 嘔吐

The drunken guy **blew chunks** all over the bathroom floor in the bar.

酒吧裡有個醉鬼，在廁所吐了滿地。

blow job

7 名 口交

The porn actress was told to perform a **blow job** on the man.

A 片女優被要求替那男的吹喇叭。

blow one's load

8 動 射精

The guy **blew his load** before the girl reached orgasm.

那女的還沒高潮，男的就先繳械了。

blow 的俚語用法非常多，彼此風馬牛不相及，要學會並記住所有的用法和使用情境，並不容易。如果用錯場合，可能會非常尷尬，所以你得特別小心，別說錯話搞砸了。

blowout [ˋbloˌaut]

1 **名** 比賽時讓對手掛蛋

The local rugby team played in a tournament against teams from the surrounding areas. The first two games were **blowouts**. The score was 10-0 and 7-0.

本地英式橄欖球隊在聯賽中和附近的隊伍較勁,前兩場比賽他們都讓對方掛蛋,比數分別是十比〇和七比〇。

2 **名** 大肆慶祝一番

There was a huge **blowout** because it was the end of the semester, and many of the expats were going home.

學期結束學生開趴狂歡,還有很多外國學生準備回家。

blow out

3 **片** **動** 爛醉如泥

Most of the people at the bar were **blown out** because they had been drinking since noon.

酒吧很多人都醉倒了,因為他們從中午就開始喝了。

4 **片** **動** 疲憊的

Stacy was so **blown out** from her camping trip that she didn't have the energy to unpack.

史黛西露營回來累死了,根本沒力氣打開行李。

blowout源於美國,除了「開派對慶祝」之外,最常描述比賽中某個隊伍整場掛零的狀況,多半是運動選手和球迷在用。

bone [bon]

1 副 瘦到皮包骨

After being out in the wilderness for so long, the man looked **bone** thin when he returned home.

那男的在荒野裡待這麼久,回家時只剩下皮包骨。

2 動 做愛

Chuck is always bragging about **boning** chicks.

恰克老是誇口自己上過多少妹。

bonehead

3 名 傻瓜、笨蛋

James always does the stupidest things. He's such a **bonehead**!

詹姆斯每次都做出一堆蠢事,真是笨蛋耶!

boner

4 名 大錯或錯誤

Steve pulled a major **boner** when he sent a message to his girlfriend via LINE, inviting her to the surprise party he'd planned for her.

史提夫幹了蠢事,居然 Line 他女友,邀她參加他幫她辦的驚喜趴。

5 名 勃起

Kenny got a **boner** in the middle of gym class when he saw the girls in their short shorts.

肯尼體育課看到女生穿熱褲,忍不住搭帳棚了。

bone up on

6 片動 苦讀或鑽研

You need to **bone up on** math if you want to get into business school.

你得苦讀數學，才能進商學院。

bone-dry

7 形 非常乾燥的

My raincoat and rain boots kept me **bone-dry** in the heavy rain.

我的雨衣、雨鞋讓我下大雨也保持乾燥。

8 形 滴酒不沾

He's been **bone-dry** ever since he gave up alcohol ten years ago.

十年前戒酒後，他就滴酒不沾了。

　　bone（骨頭）這個堅硬的鈣化組織怎麼會衍生出這麼多不同的用法？bone 和 blow 一樣，如果用錯了，你自己就成了不折不扣的 **bonehead**（笨蛋）！

　　boner 表示「愚蠢、明顯的錯誤」或「勃起的老二」。

　　bone-dry 像骨頭暴露於空氣中，用來形容「非常乾燥」。另一個意思是指「滴酒不沾」，形容人拒絕任何含有酒精的飲料。

bop [bɑp]

1 ⓥ 快速、放鬆地動

People in the audience were **bopping** their heads to the beat of the music.

觀眾區的人隨著音樂節拍點頭。

2 ⓥ 打

The two kids kept **bopping** each other over the head with their toys.

那兩個小孩一直拿玩具打對方的頭。

3 ⓥ 跳舞

People who have no rhythm can still enjoy **bopping** on the dance floor.

沒節奏感的人還是可以在舞池裡自由跳舞。

bop 描述「人移動」或「擊打他人」。bop on the dance floor 表示你在舞池裡「輕鬆、迅速地動」。

bounce [baʊns]

1 🔊 電子郵件無法送達，退回給寄件人

For some reason, the emails I send you keep **bouncing** back.
不知為什麼，我寄給你的電子郵件都被退信了。

2 🔊 支票被退，因為開票人戶頭裡的存款不足

The check that Jenny wrote to pay for the purchase **bounced**.
珍妮購物開的支票被退票。

3 🔊 恢復

Irene knew she had to **bounce** back and move on with her life.
艾琳知道她應該要回到正軌，繼續過生活。

4 🔊 被開除或被趕出某個地方

Jack got caught stealing important information from work and was **bounced** from his job immediately!
傑克被抓到盜取工作的重要資料，馬上就被掃地出門了！

The two men were **bounced** from the nightclub after they got into a fight.
那兩人跟人打起來以後，就被轟出夜店了。

bounce 原意是「彈跳」，俚語用法大多也和這樣的動作有關，像是「電子郵件被退回給寄件人」、「支票無法兌現被退票」、「恢復正常生活步調」，或是「開除、被逼走」，都當動詞用。

box [bɑks]

1 名 棺材

Many people end up in a **box** at a young age as a result of gang violence.

因為幫派暴力，很多人年紀輕輕就躺進棺材了。

2 名 保險箱

Many bank robbers go for what's in the **box**, not just the money behind the counter.

很多銀行搶匪不只要櫃檯裡的錢，還想要保險箱裡的東西。

3 名 電視

Are there any good programs on the **box** this evening?

晚上有什麼好電視節目可以看嗎？

4 名 女性生殖器

Don't let just any guy get into your **box**.

不要隨便讓男生碰妳的 B（屄）。

　　box 也是一個有很多不同意義的字，原指「有堅硬外殼的盒子或箱子」。當作俚語時，可指「棺材」、「保險箱」、「電視」或「女性生殖器」。什麼情境下代表什麼意思，應該不難區別。

　　box 指「電視」，是英式用法，指「女性生殖器」源自澳洲，但是在西半球也用得非常普遍，不過這樣的說法比較低俗，大多數人都不會在公開場合使用這個字。大多是男生在談論想要進入女性私處時使用，女性通常不會使用這個字。

bucket [ˈbʌkɪt]

1 動 快速移動

The car **bucketed** down the highway and almost hit a truck.
那輛車在高速公路上飆車，差點撞到卡車。

in buckets

2 慣 下大雨

As we were eating on the patio at the restaurant it began to rain **in buckets**.
我們坐在餐廳露台吃飯時，天空開始下起傾盆大雨來。

kick the bucket

3 慣 死

The man finally **kicked the bucket** at the ripe age of 97.
那個人最終死於高齡 97 歲。

　　bucket原來是「水桶」的意思，當作俚語時它有兩個不同的意義，而且在英國和美國的用法不太一樣。

　　在美國，bucket 用來指「快速移動」。在英國 in buckets用來指「下大雨」。

　　kick the bucket指「死」，其來源可能是以前的人要上吊是在站水桶上，再把水桶踢掉自殺，因此引申為「死」。

023

012 ▶

buff [bʌf]

1 名 ……狂或……迷

Peter is an indie music **buff**. His CD collection is quite impressive.

彼得是獨立音樂迷，他的 CD 收藏很壯觀。

2 形 強壯、健康、性感的

My roommate John is the **buffest** guy I know in Taipei.

我的室友約翰是我在台北認識最健美的男生。

3 名 赤裸

Mandy took a late night ocean swim in the **buff**.

曼蒂深夜跑去海裡裸泳。

　　buff 原意是「暗黃色」，當俚語時有很多意義，包括「……狂」、「健壯性感的」或「赤裸」，和原意一點關聯都沒有。

　　這是個輕鬆有趣的字，所以你不太可能因為這個字出什麼大錯，不過如果你想告訴對方你有多迷什麼，卻告訴對方你是光著身子的，那就尷尬了！

bust [bʌst]

1 名 查獲毒品

The police seized a hundred kilograms of cocaine during a recent drug **bust**.

最近一次緝毒行動中，警察查緝了一百公斤的古柯鹼。

2 動 越獄

The prisoner **busted** out of prison by digging a tunnel from his cell.

犯人在牢房挖了一條地道成功越獄。

3 動 取笑

Steve was always **bustin'** on Mike for not having a girlfriend.

史提夫老是笑麥可沒女朋友。

4 動 很會跳舞

That girl on the dance floor can really **bust** a move.

舞池裡那女孩很會跳舞。

5 動 查出、發現真相

When Emily saw Richard out with another girl, she knew she had **busted** him for the last time. She simply wasn't going to put up with it anymore.

艾蜜莉看到理查在和別的女生約會時，就知道這是她最後一次抓到他，她再也不要這樣默默忍受了。

buster

6 **名** 男人或男孩

When her son tried to get away with doing something he knew he shouldn't, Jane would stop him and say, "Not so fast there, **buster**."

珍的兒子知道自己做了不該做的事，想偷溜，珍就會攔下他，說：「別跑這麼快啊，小子。」

7 **名** 馴馬師

The ranch owner hired a **buster** to help with the wild mares he had on the ranch.

牧場主人雇用了馴馬師，幫他訓練農場裡那些母野馬。

　　bust 當動詞時，原意是「打破」、「爆裂」；當名詞時，原來是指「胸像、半身像」，或是「人的胸部」，特別是女性的胸部。

　　它當俚語使用時，意義多是負面的，而且和原意也沒什麼關聯，最常用來指「查獲毒品」、「越獄」和「取笑」。

buzz [bʌz]

1 名 抽完大麻之後的愉悅感

I'm still feeling the **buzz** from that joint.
我吸完大麻，還在飄飄欲仙。

2 名 興奮感

At the beginning of a new relationship, you often feel this strong **buzz** every time the two of you are together.
戀愛初期，每次兩人在一起，常常心裡小鹿亂撞。

3 名 謠言

There is always a **buzz** about who did what and who is dating whom. 總是有謠言說誰做了什麼，或是誰跟誰在約會。

buzzkill

4 名 掃興的人事物

Every time I feel good about something, Debra always has to say something negative to bring me down. She's such a **buzzkill**.
每當我很嗨，黛柏拉老愛講話潑我冷水，她真的很掃興。

　　buzz 原是擬聲詞，如蜜蜂的嗡嗡聲或電動刮鬍刀的聲音，當俚語時，形容吸大麻或是喝醉酒後，輕飄飄、茫茫的興奮感。
　　buzz 也指「內心的興奮」，有新事發生時的興奮感；另指「謠言或八卦」。
　　buzzkill 則是用來表示什麼事讓你覺得很掃興。

014

can [kæn]

1 名 廁所

Jim had to go to the bathroom so bad that he ran to the **can** the minute he got back to the house.
吉姆尿急，一到家馬上就衝進廁所。

2 名 監獄或牢房

If you get caught committing a crime, you will be thrown in the **can**.
如果你犯了罪，就會被關進大牢。

3 動 監禁某人

On his way home from the party, Bill got **canned** for drinking and driving. 派對結束回家路上，比爾因酒駕被捕。

4 動 開除

Lisa was **canned** because she didn't show up for work for a week. 麗莎整個禮拜沒去上班，最後被開除了。

　　can 原指「裝飲料或食物的金屬密封罐」，最常用的俚語是「廁所」和「監禁」，以前沒廁所，大家靠挖洞或金屬容器來解決大小便，而後 can 代稱廁所。監牢跟罐頭一樣狹窄，金屬環繞四周，因此 can 代指監獄。

　　這兩種用法並不正式，使用 can 的人通常教育程度較低；較年長的一代可能並不了解「廁所」和「監獄」這些新用法。

chicken [ˈtʃɪkɪn]

1 名 膽小鬼、懦夫

The last time Dave asked me to go skydiving with him, I refused. He's been calling me a **chicken** ever since.

上次戴夫問我要不要跟他去高空跳傘，我拒絕以後，他就開始叫我膽小鬼。

2 形 膽小的

I am **chicken** when it comes to heights.

每次到高的地方，我就很膽小。

chicken out

3 慣 臨陣退縮

John was going to go bungee jumping but **chickened out** at the last minute.

約翰本來要高空彈跳，但是最後一刻臨陣退縮了。

 大概是因為有什麼風吹草動，雞都會被驚動，所以 **chicken** 就用來形容一遇到事情就害怕的人，而形容害怕想脫逃的行為就可以用 **chicken out**。

cool [kul]

1 形 冷靜

When Jane got pulled over by customs officers at the border, she tried to remain **cool** to avoid getting busted.

珍在邊境被海關攔下來的時候試圖保持鎮定,以免被抓。

2 形 最棒的、最酷的

That was the **coolest** concert I've ever seen! The band, the stage, the lighting, and the crowd were all awesome!

那真是我看過最酷的演唱會!樂團、舞台、燈光和人群都讚透了!

3 形 有趣的

Dan wanted to learn photography because he thought that it would be a **cool** hobby.

丹想學攝影,因為他覺得那是個有趣的嗜好。

4 形 可以接受的

I don't mind if Zach moves into our apartment as long as the other guys are **cool** with having a fourth roommate.

只要其他人可以接受再多一個室友,我不介意札克搬進公寓。

cool 也是一個多年來反覆流行的字,意義沒變過,從五〇年代末、六〇年代初期就開始有人使用這個字了,似乎每一代都有一段時期流行用 cool,還有其他表達「酷」的新字陸續出現,但cool 是一個你一輩子都可以使用的字。

crap [kræp]

1 名 屎

Brian had to take a massive **crap** because he ate too much.

布萊恩剛吃太多，得拉一大坨屎。

2 名 垃圾、廢物

My computer shut down by itself again. What a piece of **crap**!

我的電腦又自己關機了，真是爛貨！

3 名 廢話、胡說

The rumor about Allie dating Steve back in December turned out to be a load of **crap**; they've never even kissed each other.

結果艾莉十二月跟史提夫約會的謠言都是胡扯，他們甚至連親嘴都沒有。

crap out

4 片 動 因為害怕而退出

Ben called Maggie and told her he wanted her to move to Asia and travel around with him, but he **crapped out** at the last minute. Now, she thinks he never really meant what he said!

班打電話給瑪姬，希望她和他一起搬去亞洲、四處遊玩，但是最後一刻他又退縮了，現在瑪姬覺得他老是說話不算話！

crap out on

5 片動 因為太累而退出某事

We're nearly finished with the project. I know you're tired but don't **crap out on** me now!

我們快完成案子了，我知道你很累，但別留我獨自面對。

crap 是粗俗的字眼，表示「屎」，英文的 feces（糞便）太正式，反而很少用，而 poo 或 number two 從小就開始用了。

crap 也可以指「垃圾」、「廢物」或是「胡扯」、「謠言」。

crap 當動詞時，負面涵義更為強烈，**crap out** 表示「因為害怕而退出某事」，而 **crap out on** 表示「因太累而退出某事」。

cream [krim]

1 動 痛扁

The obnoxious drunk guy at the bar was talking so much crap that a bunch of guys **creamed** him as he was leaving the bar.

酒吧裡討厭的醉鬼胡扯了一大堆，結果走時被一群男的海扁一頓。

2 動 射精

The guy was watching a porno movie and **creamed** his underwear.

那個男的在看 A 片，結果射得內褲上都是。

3 動 讓對手慘敗

The Philadelphia 76ers **creamed** the L.A. Lakers in overtime.

費城 76 人隊在延長賽中大敗洛杉磯湖人隊。

cream 本意是「奶油」，俚語和原意並無直接關聯。雖然它原來是個名詞，也無褒貶之義，但當俚語時卻全都當動詞用，且都具有負面意義。cream 可指「讓對方慘敗」，但是並不常用。

cunt [kʌnt]

1 **名 女性的陰部**

Referring to a woman's sexual organ as a **cunt** is extremely offensive.

把女生的陰部叫作「雞掰」，超沒禮貌的。

2 **名 女人**

In a moment of drunken rage, he called the woman a **cunt**.

發酒瘋的時候，他把女人叫作「賤屄」。

3 **名 可鄙、卑劣的人**

Greg is such a lying **cunt** for having cheated on his wife all these years.

格瑞格偷吃了好幾年，騙人的爛貨。

4 **名 笨蛋、白痴**

Liz usually avoids using vulgar words, but she was so angry at Stephanie for what she had done that she called her a **cunt** to her face.

麗茲通常不會爆粗口，但是她很氣史蒂芬妮的作為，所以當面罵她白痴！

cunt 指「女性陰部」，是非常粗俗的用法，非常負面，醫學界並不用這個字。英國用 cunt 罵人笨蛋，但在美國，cunt 罵人很可惡，在美國 cunt 可是件嚴重的事，要小心使用。

018

D

032

deadhead ['dɛd,hɛd]

1 名 搖滾樂團「死之華」的死忠粉絲

My friend Marc was such a **Deadhead** that he would follow the band around while they toured the country. However, he stopped after Jerry Garcia died.

我朋友馬克是「死之華」的死忠粉絲，全國巡演時他狂追，後來主唱傑利·賈西亞死了，他才沒繼續追。

2 名 蠢蛋

Bill drank a lot and because of this, he never finished school. He was such a **deadhead** compared to the rest of his friends.

比爾因為酗酒，結果畢不了業，和朋友比起來，他真是個蠢蛋。

3 動 開空車或空機

The truck carried goods to California and then **deadheaded** back to the East Coast.

這卡車載貨到加州，再空車開回東岸。

看到 **deadhead**，人們最常想到的就是 Grateful Dead（死之華搖滾樂團），狂追死之華樂團的死忠粉絲被稱作 Deadhead，他們可是對這個稱號很自豪的。雖然主唱傑利·賈西亞（Jerry Garcia）1995 年去世了，他們的音樂依然和以往一樣受人喜愛。

deadhead 另外一個最重要的俚語意義就是「愚蠢」或「無聊」的人，這些人腦袋像死了一樣（dead head）！

deck [dεk]

1 图 滑板

Tony Hawk, a famous skateboarder, designs his own **decks**. He has some really sweet board designs.

知名滑板手東尼‧霍克自己設計滑板，有些設計還真不賴。

2 图 衝浪板

It's always best to wear a rash guard when surfing, so that when you rub against the **deck** of the board it doesn't irritate your skin.

衝浪的時候最好穿潛水裝，這樣身體摩擦到衝浪板，才不會刺激皮膚。

3 图 一包毒品

When the cops busted the drug dealer, he had at least 20 **decks** on him.

那名毒販被警察抓到的時候，身上至少有 20 包毒品。

4 動 把人打倒在地

A fan from the visitor's team came and sat down in the home team section. When he started to talk shit about the home team, he got **decked**.

一名客場球隊的球迷跑來坐在主場球隊區，開始批評主場球隊，結果就被揍趴了。

deck 原意指「一疊撲克牌」、「船的甲板」或「屋子側門旁邊的木製平台」。deck 當俚語時可指「滑板或衝浪板」、「一包毒品」，還可以用來形容「把人打倒在地」，多用於年輕一代，原意則是老一輩在用。

deep six ['dip 'sıks]

1 動 埋葬某人

If you decide that you don't want to be **deep sixed** after you die, you could choose to be cremated instead.

如果你死後不想土葬，可以選擇火化。

2 動 丟棄、毀滅

I recommend that you **deep six** all your old documents and bills with a paper shredder.

我建議你把舊文件和帳單用碎紙機銷毀。

 葬禮時埋葬死者的深度一般是六英呎，因此 **deep six** 指人去世後被埋在地底下的深度，只當俚語用，所以當你有什麼秘密不想被發現的時候，也可以 deep six（銷毀）它，深深埋起來。

dick [dɪk]

1 名 老二

The word penis sounds funny and makes Amber laugh, so she just says **dick** instead.

「陰莖」聽起來很搞笑，每次都讓安柏笑個不停，所以她都說「老二」，不說「陰莖」。

2 名 笨蛋；討厭鬼

Monty can be a real **dick** when he's drunk. He'll often start insulting the bartender and the people around him.

蒙提每次喝醉就變成大混蛋，常常對酒保和坐他旁邊的人爆粗口。

3 名 什麼都沒有

You don't know **dick** about what I'm going through, so stop giving me advice.

我的狀況，你懂個屁啦，別再給我建議了。

dickhead

4 名 混蛋

Any time Jackie gets mad at a driver for cutting across her lane, she calls him a **dickhead**.

每次潔姬被超車，就會氣得大罵對方混蛋。

dick around

Instead of looking for a job, Adam just **dicks around** at home all day.

亞當不去找工作，整天家裡蹲。

one's dick in one's hand

Don't just stand there with **your dick in your hand**. Help me move this sofa.

不要站在那邊閒閒沒事，來幫我搬沙發。

dick 所有俚語用法都很粗俗，最常見的用法指男生的「老二」；dick 專門用來罵男生，罵女生則多用 airhead。

having your dick in your hand 意思是「什麼也不做，很沒用」。

dip [dɪp]

1

名 豬頭

Samantha can be such a **dip** sometimes; last night she left the gas burner on by accident.

莎曼珊有時候真的很豬頭，昨晚竟然不小心讓瓦斯爐開著。

2

動 閃人、突然離開

This party is boring. Let's **dip** the hell out of here.

這趴無聊到爆，我們閃人吧！

Roy **dipped** when he saw the police approaching.

羅伊看到警察靠近，就閃人了。

　　dip 原來當作動詞用，意思是「拿東西沾某種液體」，動作通常都很快。俚語當名詞時，意指「豬頭」；當動詞時，意指「突然離開」。

dish [dɪʃ]

1 名 迷人的女性或男性

It is kind of odd these days to hear a guy call an attractive girl a **dish**. It's something my grandfather would say.

現在男生把「美眉」叫作「佳人」有點怪了，這比較像是我爺爺說的話。

2 名 閒聊、八卦

What's going on between Jane and her boyfriend Matt? Come on, give me the latest **dish**!

阿珍和她男友麥特怎麼了？快爆最新八卦給我聽！

3 動 擊敗、毀壞

The Sharks got **dished** by the Cats during Saturday night's game. 鯊魚隊星期六晚上的比賽被野貓隊痛宰。

dish out

4 片 動 散佈

Lynn is the type of person who could **dish out** criticism but never take it herself. 琳恩老是愛批人，但受不了被批。

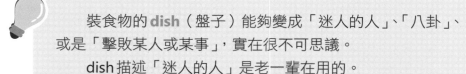

　　裝食物的 **dish**（盤子）能夠變成「迷人的人」、「八卦」、或是「擊敗某人或某事」，實在很不可思議。

　　dish 描述「迷人的人」是老一輩在用的。

　　dish 表「謠言」、「八卦」是一個禮貌但稍微過時的說法。

　　如果有人想 dish 你，你最好不要呆呆地站在那裡，因為這裡的 dish 是「擊倒」的意思。

dog [dɔg]

1 名 熱狗

At baseball games, Roy likes to get a soda and a **dog** during the seventh inning stretch.

看棒球賽時，羅伊一定會在第七局中場休息時，去買點汽水和熱狗。

2 名 淫亂的男人

My buddy tries to take a different girl home from the bar every weekend. He is such a **dog**!

我哥們每週末都從酒吧帶不同的女生回家，真是條野狗！

dog days

3 名 夏季最熱的時候

During the **dog days** of summer, many people try to stay cool by heading to the mountains.

夏天最熱的那段時間，很多人上山避暑納涼。

　　人類最好的朋友 dog（狗）居然有這麼多種的俚語用法，實在很有趣。dog 可指食物「熱狗」，也可把「淫亂的男人」比作狗，因為他們充滿獸慾。

　　用 dog days 形容夏季最熱的天氣，是因為北半球七月初到八月初，天狼星（Dog Star）這段時間跟太陽同時升落，因此將這段夏季天氣最熱的時期稱為 dog days。

dope [dop]

1 名 笨蛋

That guy is such a **dope**. He couldn't answer even one question in the exam.

那個男的真是個笨蛋，他考試連半題都答不出來。

2 名 毒品

The man got arrested for possession of **dope**.

那男的因持有毒品被捕。

3 名 資訊

Give me the **dope** on the camping trip; then I'll decide if I want to go with you guys.

把露營的資訊告訴我，我再決定要不要跟你們去。

4 形 很酷的

That new surfboard Sophia got is so **dope**! I wish I had my own deck!

蘇菲亞新買的衝浪板好酷哦！我真希望我也有一個！

字典裡所列的 **dope** 都是俚語用法，dope 是「毒品」的暱稱，在美國通常指海洛因，比較不指大麻。

近年來在美國 dope 也產生了新的意義，如：

Give me the dope. 把相關資訊告訴我。

I need to know what the dope is! 我得搞清楚狀況！

dope 也指「很酷」，但是老實說，還用 dope 說「酷」的人一點都不酷。

drill [drɪl]

1 ⑧ 正常程序、正確步驟

Let's go over the **drill** so that we don't make any mistakes: When I give the signal, Jeff turns out the light, Sue opens the door, and when Pete walks in, we all yell "Surprise!"

我們再走一次流程吧，這樣才不會犯錯：當我給暗號，傑夫關燈，阿蘇開門，當彼特進來，我們就大喊「驚喜」。

2 ⑩ 上；性交

Do you see that girl over there? Martin **drilled** her last night.

你看到那邊那個女生了嗎？馬丁昨晚上她了。

 drill 的原意是「鑽洞」或「鑽子」，它當作俚語用時，可以指「做愛」，是很粗野的說法。

drop [drɑp]

1 動 分手

Christine was so tired of her boyfriend's behavior that she decided to **drop** him.

克莉斯汀受夠了男友的行為，所以決定甩了他。

2 動 告知

Jen **dropped** a bomb when she told everyone that she was pregnant. 珍跟大家說她懷孕的時候，真的把大家嚇了一大跳。

3 動 把人打倒在地

A guy at the bar said some rude things to me, and my boyfriend **dropped** him on the spot, in front of everyone.

酒吧裡有個男的對我爆粗口，我男友立刻當眾把他揍趴。

4 動 口服毒品

At the club, Janis saw some people **dropping** ecstasy in the bathroom before going back out to the dance floor.

珍妮絲上完廁所準備回舞池，看到有幾個人在嗑搖頭丸。

5 名 進行非法交易的場所

The cops knew where the **drop** was supposed to take place, but they weren't sure if they'd be able to arrest the drug smugglers.

警方知道毒品交易的地點，但是不確定能不能抓到毒品走私販。

　　　drop 原意指「水滴」，雖然原意以名詞為主，它的俚語意義卻多當動詞，指「分手」、「告知」、「把人打倒在地」、「口服毒品」。它唯一的名詞用法為「進行非法交易的場所」。

042

dump [dʌmp]

1 名 骯髒破舊的地方

It's no fun living with a bunch of slobs. Our apartment looks like a **dump** most of the time.

跟一群懶鬼住一起不好玩，我們的公寓常常像豬窩一樣。

2 名 屎

"Where's Ted?"

"He'll be right back. He went to take a **dump**."

「泰德去哪了？」

「他去拉屎了，等等就回來了。」

3 動 拋棄

Michelle's boyfriend **dumped** her for another woman.

米雪兒的男友為了另一個女人把她甩掉。

dump on

4 動 批評、責罵

Sarah is always **dumping on** Chris for the way he looks and behaves.

莎拉老是愛批評克里斯的樣子和行為。

 不管在什麼狀況下，我都不想和 **dump** 或 **dump on** 扯上關係。不管你是住在「豬窩」裡、得上「大號」、被人「批評」或「甩掉」，都不是件好事，dump 是個負面的字。

easy [ˋizɪ]

1 ⑱ 隨和的

"What do you want to do this weekend?" "You decide. I'm **easy**."

「你週末想幹啥？」「你決定啦，我都行。」

2 ⑱ 隨便的（跟人上床）

A guy who wants a one-night stand wants a girl who is **easy** but a guy who wants a serious relationship doesn't want a girl like that!

想要一夜情的男生，都想找個隨便跟別人上床的女生，但是想要認真談戀愛的男生，可不想要這種女生！

3 ⑱ 毫不擔心的

I never feel **easy** around Louise. She seems to get offended by everything I say.

我跟露易絲相處都超挫的，好像我說什麼都會冒犯她。

4 ⑱ 冷靜

Easy now. I'm not going to tell you the whole story if you're going to get upset and do something you'll regret later.

冷靜點，如果你生氣或做出什麼會後悔的事，我就不跟你說整件事了。

　　不困難、不複雜的東西就是 **easy**，也就是你能夠毫不費力就達到你的目標。它的俚語意義也相當類似，如果說你很 easy，可能有兩個意義：一是你是很隨和，什麼都好；二是你沒什麼道德，隨隨便便就跟人上床。

ear candy [ˈɪr ˈkændɪ]

1 名 輕鬆悅耳的音樂

I'm not in the mood to listen to deep music. Put on some **ear candy** instead.

我現在沒心情聽什麼有深度的音樂，放一點洗腦歌吧！

2 名 欣賞的口音

I love Jean-Philippe's French accent. It's pure **ear candy**.

我喜歡尚菲利普的法國口音，超好聽。

　　ear candy 可不能照字面解，吃糖讓人心情愉快，在 candy 前加個 ear，表示聽起來讓人愉快的事物，通常是指「愉快悅耳的音樂」，沒有複雜的結構和深度；ear candy 也可以形容「好聽的腔調和口音」。下次聽到 ear candy 可不要以為它是一種吃的糖果哦！

fart [fɑrt]

1 名 放屁

The room was quiet because everyone was studying for the test. Then all of a sudden, Patrick let out a loud **fart** and everyone started to laugh.

教室裡鴉雀無聲，全班都在準備考試。突然之間，派屈克放了一聲響屁，每個人都笑出來。

2 名 可鄙、卑劣的人

Mr. Heckles was such an old **fart**. He was always complaining to the landlord about his neighbors' making too much noise. The truth is that they weren't loud; he just liked to complain.

哈克斯先生真是小人，每次都跟房東抱怨鄰居太吵，其實鄰居根本就不吵，他只是愛抱怨。

fart about / fart around

3 片 動 鬼混

On Saturday afternoon, Jessie and Amanda **farted about/around** Queen Anne, their favorite part of town.

星期六下午，潔西和阿曼達常跑去安妮皇后區鬼混，她們最愛那一區了。

有些人光是發出 **fart** 的音就會忍不住笑出來，有些人則永遠都不會開口說 fart，它不算是髒話，但還是有人覺得不禮貌，你可以在輕鬆的對話中使用 fart 和 fart about。

fire up [ˋfaɪr ˏʌp]

1 片動 生氣、憤怒

The teacher got **fired up** when she caught Johnny cheating for the second time this term.

老師氣炸了，這學期她第二次抓到強尼作弊。

2 片動 很興奮

Mary was so **fired up** about her summer vacation. She had been planning it for almost six months.

講到暑假，瑪莉就超興奮的，她計畫了將近半年了。

3 片動 性慾高漲

The sexy little dance routine that Allie did for her boyfriend for his birthday really **fired** him **up**.

艾利的男友生日，她跳了一小段豔舞，讓他血脈賁張。

4 片動 吸毒後很興奮

Dana was totally **fired up** after snorting coke all night long.

戴娜吸了古柯鹼後，整夜都超嗨的。

5 片動 喝醉的

The guys at the pub were **fired up** from drinking pints and watching rugby.

酒吧裡的男生邊看英式橄欖球賽，邊喝酒，都喝茫了。

fire up 指強烈情緒，像是生氣、興奮或性興奮。這些感覺很像熊熊烈火一發不可收拾，讓人「著火」! fire up 是個充滿情緒的字眼，因此當你興奮得不得了時可以這麼說！

fix [fɪks]

1 動 報仇，通常是殺人

Tony is a mob boss, so if anyone messes with his family, he'll have them **fixed**.

東尼是黑社會老大，誰敢找他家人麻煩，都會被他做掉。

2 動 施打毒品

The junkie needed a **fix** to help him get through the night.

這個毒蟲需要來一針，才能撐到天亮。

3 動 在比賽中做手腳

Some believe that big sporting events are **fixed** to guarantee huge wins to those who bet big money on games.

有些人相信大型體育賽事有幕後操盤，保證那些下大注的人贏大錢。

4 名 興奮感

The excitement of winning is the **fix** that pushes many professional athletes to compete.

贏得比賽的那份興奮感，驅使很多專業運動員繼續比賽。

5 名 尷尬的處境

Debbie got herself into a real **fix** when she promised to give a speech at the charity event and then realized she had to leave for Brazil that same day.

黛比答應慈善活動要演講，結果發現那天要出國去巴西，真囧。

如果東西壞了，就需要修理，這是 **fix** 的原意，當俚語時，表示「改善情況」，但手段可能不合法。

flake [flek]

1 **名 怪人**

Sometimes Jessie can be such a **flake** with her weird ideas and odd behavior. 潔西有時有些怪點子和怪行為，真是怪咖。

2 **名 不可靠的人**

Cindy is a **flake**. She had said she'd go to the movies with me on Saturday, but then made plans with some other person.

辛蒂沒信用，她說週六要跟我看電影，結果又跟別人有約。

flake out

3 **片 動 累垮**

After staying up all night with friends, Michelle **flaked out** on the couch. She was too tired to even walk to her bed.

跟朋友熬了一夜沒睡，蜜雪兒累癱在沙發上，甚至連回床上睡都沒力。

flaky

4 **形 瘋瘋癲癲的**

Back then, the scientist's ideas seemed **flaky**; however, as time passed, people began to realize that his ideas were ahead of his time. 從前這個科學家被認為很瘋狂，後來時間久了，大家才明白他的想法超時代了。

如果你是 **flake**，表示你是「怪咖」，不過這只是個人意見，並非醫學診斷，**flaky** 是形容詞，表「瘋狂的、古怪的」。如果你 **flake out**，就表示你「累垮」了。

flip [flɪp]

1 形 輕率的、無禮的

His **flip** remarks annoyed everyone and showed that he didn't really care about what others thought of him.

他說話輕率讓大家不爽，他根本不在乎別人怎麼想他。

flip (out)

2 片動 勃然大怒

OK, Katie. Everything is going to be all right. Don't **flip out**.

好啦，凱蒂，沒事了，別發火。

3 片動 情緒爆發

The sight of the damaged car **flipped** Lucy **out**, as she thought about how much it would cost to get it fixed.

露西見到車子受損的樣子，快爆炸了，因為她想到要花大錢才能修好車。

　　先別激動！每次你用 flip 或 flip out，或者是別人把這個字用在你身上時，就表示有人或有事惹你不高興了。flip 的原意是「翻面」，俚語用法和原意頗有雷同之處，就好像你本來心情平靜，一眨眼就換了另一種心情。

freak [frik]

1 名 對……狂熱的人

Some of the people I know can be real religious **freaks**, and I feel a bit uncomfortable being around them.

我認識一些人是宗教狂熱分子，跟他們在一起我覺得有點不自在。

freak (out)

2 片動 失控、崩潰

When Stacy found out Scott had cheated on her, she **freaked**!

發現史考特劈腿，史戴西抓狂了！

Even the smallest thing would **freak** Genie **out** and make her cry.

就算最小的事都會讓吉妮崩潰大哭。

3 片動 嚇壞

Seeing Rob lying there on the hospital bed with tubes up his nose really **freaked** me **out**.

看到羅柏躺在醫院床上，鼻子插著管子真是把我嚇死了。

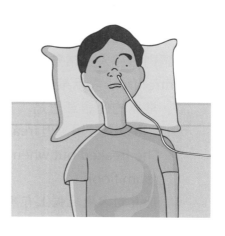

freaky

4 形 嚇人的

I've been having some **freaky** nightmares lately. Sometimes, I even wake up in the middle of the night in a cold sweat.

我最近常做恐怖的惡夢，有時半夜醒來，嚇得我一身冷汗。

　　freak 的俚語非常常見，本義是「奇怪的念頭」，俚語當名詞則形容人非常熱衷某物，到了不正常的狀態，例如常用 control freak 表示某人很喜歡控制別人，「控制狂」。

　　常見的俚語意思是「抓狂」和「嚇壞」。**freak** 和 **freak out** 常可以交替用，但 freak out 較常用在受驚嚇時，如：

She freaked out when she saw the dead rat on her living room floor.

她看到客廳地板上有死老鼠，嚇死了！

fresh [frɛʃ]

1 形 輕鬆愉快的

The runway model's outfit looked **fresh** and perfect for the summer season.

伸展台上模特兒穿的衣服看起來好清新自然，很適合夏天。

2 形 毛手毛腳的

When Gina was out shopping, an older man tried to get **fresh** with her. She was a bit freaked out by the situation.

吉娜逛街時，一個老男人想對她毛手毛腳，她當時實在氣到不行。

　　fresh 原意指「新鮮的」，俚語用法可指「輕鬆愉快的事物」，常用來描述清新自然的衣服。

　　fresh 表「毛手毛腳的」，用法源於美國，通常是指受到陌生人肢體上的性騷擾。

fuck [fʌk]

1 動 做愛

Last night, my girlfriend wanted to make love, but I was more in the mood to **fuck**.

昨晚我女朋友想要愛愛，但我比較想操她。

fuck around

2 片 動 做無謂的事

Stop **fucking around**. We have a lot of work to do.

不要再混來混去了，我們有一堆工作要做。

fuck off

3 片 動 走開、滾開

This weird man at the park wouldn't leave Trista alone so she told him to **fuck off**.

公園裡那個怪叔叔一直纏著翠斯塔，所以翠斯塔叫他滾開。

fuck up

4 片 動 搞砸

Isabella couldn't help herself. She always had to tell her boyfriend when he **fucked up**!

伊莎貝拉控制不了自己，每次她男友搞砸事情，她都要唸！

fucked

5 形 遭受嚴重損害；處境困難

Jenny is completely **fucked**! She just lost the report she had been working on because her computer suddenly crashed, and her boss wants the report tomorrow.

珍妮死定了，電腦突然壞掉，一直在趕的報告不見了，而老闆明天就要。

motherfucker

6 名 不要臉的傢伙、混球

Jeremy is such a **motherfucker**! He had been dating Emily as well as two other girls on the side for almost a year, and not one of the girls knew about the other.

傑瑞米真是他媽的混蛋！他不但跟艾蜜莉約會，又劈腿兩個女生，還將近快一年，三個女生都不知道對方的存在。

　　fuck 可能是世上最常用到的字之一，這個字粗俗無禮，是禁忌，你絕不會對長輩說，而他們也絕不會對你說。

　　有些人滿嘴 fuck，有些人發誓絕不出口「F 字」。不管是在世界上的哪個角落，只要你說出英文的 fuck，大家都會轉頭看你，所以絕對要小心使用。

　　fuck 可當動詞、名詞和形容詞，不管你用不用，它還是很有趣，能夠表達出這麼多不同的情緒。如果你還沒說過，也許可以考慮用一次看看！

053

funky ['fʌŋkɪ]

1 形 有臭味的

Kim threw away the tuna salad that was in the refrigerator because it was starting to smell **funky**.

阿金把冰箱的鮪魚沙拉丟了，因為開始發臭了。

2 形 放克風格的

This music has a **funky** rhythm that's fun to dance to.

這音樂很有節奏感，跳起舞來很好玩。

funky 表示什麼東西散發「臭味」。

funky 也是一種簡單且節奏感強烈的音樂，叫放克音樂（funk），重拍，適合跳舞。

G

030

gab [gæb]

1 名 說話

Tom has lots of great ideas that would benefit companies, but he doesn't have the gift of **gab** to market his ideas.

湯姆有很多對公司有利的好點子，但沒有推銷這些想法的口才。

2 動 閒扯

Diane has been **gabbing** on the phone for the past hour. Doesn't she have something more important to do?

黛安講電話已經長舌了一小時，她沒別的要事可做嗎？

gabfest

3 名 聚會聊天

The weekly dinners with my girlfriends always turn into **gabfests** after we've had a few bottles of wine.

我跟女性好友每週晚餐聚會喝完幾瓶酒以後，就開始哈啦個沒完。

> gab（話多）不一定是壞事，只要你找到同道中人就好。最糟的是一個人講個不停，另一個人卻只是呆坐在那裡。
> gabfest 是大家聚在一起聊是非、八卦、新聞，閒言閒語個不停。

gear [gɪr]

1 名 毒品

Hey, Matt. Can you hook me up with some **gear**?

嘿，麥特，你可以幫我牽線買毒品嗎？

2 名 衣服或配件

I have to go home and pack up my **gear**. I'm leaving for my vacation early tomorrow morning.

我得回家收拾行李，明天一大早要出發去度假。

3 名 高檔貨

My friend is such a snob. She refuses to shop anywhere that doesn't sell designer **gear**.

我朋友真勢利，不賣高檔設計品牌的地方她不去。

4 名 贓物

A lot of my friends got their bikes stolen recently. It turned out a group of people were taking the **gears** and reselling them.

最近很多朋友的腳踏車被偷，原來有一群人在收購、轉賣贓車。

gear 最常見的用法就是「衣服或配件」，不過買賣毒品、贓物或高檔貨時也可能會用到，每個工作環境或社會群體都會有某些特殊的行話或俚語，gear 便是一例。1960 年代，gear 是時尚界的用字，後來被普遍使用，當時毒蟲、囚犯等也用 gear 來代稱大麻、海洛因等毒品。

geek [gik]

1 名 電腦狂人

Mike, a computer **geek**, likes to write programs in his spare time.
麥克是電腦狂人，他有空時就愛寫程式。

2 名 害羞、跟不上流行、話少的人

Eric was a real **geek** in high school, but now that he's in college, he's become quite popular with the girls.
艾瑞克高中時是個怪胎，但上了大學後變得很受女生歡迎。

geek out

3 片 動 行為古怪

Annie **geeks out** every time the guy she has a crush on comes over and speaks to her.
每次安妮暗戀的男生來跟她講話，她就有點反常。

geek 就是體育課最後一名，自己一個人吃午餐，或是放學後騎腳踏車回家時，騎在公車前面的人，這些人的行為古怪，也不擅長社交，對流行沒什麼感覺。

現在 geek 更常用來形容對電腦和網路科技有狂熱興趣的人，computer geek 就是指電腦怪才，電腦技能相當厲害。

get it together

1 慣 有組織、有系統

If you don't **get it together**, you will lose your job!

如果你做事沒組織，會丟掉工作的！

get it through one's head

2 慣 了解

I don't know how many times I have to tell you before you **get it through your head**! 我真不知道要講幾遍你才懂！

get it on

3 慣 做愛

After the club, Erin and I went back to my place and we **got it on**. 艾琳和我離開酒吧以後，就去我家打炮了。

get it up

4 慣 勃起

Jake was so drunk that he wasn't able to **get it up** with his girlfriend. 傑克喝掛了，結果到他女友家之後老二站不起來。

最常用的是 **get it together** 和 **get it through one's head**。**get it on** 有點下流，有搞笑意味。

get loose

1 片動 放鬆

Before we begin exercising, let's **get loose** by shaking out our arms and legs.

運動前,我們先動動手腳,放鬆一下。

2 片動 跳舞、享樂

Kathy was really stressed, so we went dancing, and after a few drinks, she was able to **get loose** on the dance floor.

凱西太緊繃了,所以我們去跳舞,幾杯酒後,她在舞池就比較放得開了。

關於 **get loose** 你唯一該知道的事,就是你應該身體力行,get loose(放鬆、享樂)能解除你所有的憂慮。你可以一個人,也可以和朋友一起 get loose;可以私底下,也可以在公眾場合 get loose。

當你覺得緊繃不安,什麼事都做不了,這時你就該去放鬆享樂一番了。這可是最好的處方喔!

get off

1 片動 幸運逃脫

The man **got off** easy this time with just a speeding ticket, but he may not be so lucky in the future.

那男的這次只被開超速紅單，以後可不一定這麼好運。

get off on

2 片動 性慾亢奮

Some people **get off on** watching live sex shows on the Internet.

有些人看網路現場直播的性愛秀會性慾高漲。

get off one's back

3 慣 別再嘮叨了

Dad, please **get off my back**. I am doing the best I can with my classes and with soccer.

爸，別唸我了，我的功課和足球都已經盡最大的努力了。

get off 是指做錯事，應該被罰卻沒被罰或只受輕罰；受輕罰可以說 get off easy 或 get off lightly，或者 get off with a small fine（只被罰一點點錢）。

get off on 表示你「性慾高漲」。

get off someone's back 表示「停止嘮叨」，這時候被唸的人可是會很開心的！

get on the ball

1 慣 更努力

OK, class. You need to **get on the ball**. You have exams coming up in two weeks and most of you aren't prepared to take them.

同學們，要振作了，你們兩週後要考試，很多人都還沒準備好。

get one's ass in gear

2 慣 準備行動

Get your ass in gear and start packing, or else we're going on this vacation without you!

動作給我快點，開始打包，要不然你別想跟我們去度假！

get real

3 慣 醒醒

You really think you'll get into Harvard with these grades? **Get real**!

你真以為你憑這種成績能進哈佛嗎？醒醒吧！

get on the ball 表示快去做該做的事，別再打混了。英式英文因發音的關係將 ass 拼寫為 arse，因此 **get one's ass/ arse in gear** 都對。

goof [guf]

1 名 犯下愚蠢錯誤的人

Walker is such a **goof**! No one takes him seriously because he's always doing stupid things at work.

沃克真是個呆頭鵝，沒人把他當一回事，因為他上班時，淨幹些蠢事。

goof up

2 片 動 犯愚蠢的錯誤

Teresa was making dinner for some friends the other day and she **goofed** (**up**) on the recipe. She added salt where she should have added sugar. It was so bad they couldn't eat the dish.

泰瑞莎前幾天做晚餐給好朋友們吃，結果犯了一個超級白痴的錯，把該加糖的加成了鹽，超難吃的，沒人吃得下去。

goof around

3 片 動 打混

My friends and I spent the afternoon just **goofing around**. We didn't do anything special.

我跟朋友一下午都在混，啥事都沒幹。

goof off

4 片動 逃避責任

Jeremy always cracks jokes and **goofs off** as a way to avoid taking responsibility for his actions.

傑瑞米老是開玩笑、裝瘋賣傻，因為他不想為自己的行為負責。

5 片動 打混

Instead of studying, Matt **goofs off** by surfing the Internet.

麥特不念書，反而上網打混。

 家長、老師常用 goof 來跟學齡階段的孩子，委婉地表示「別越搞越糟」，當然你還是可以用 goof 跟大人說，別搞砸了！

green [grin]

1 形 環保的

We tried to use only **green** products and materials in building our house.

我們試著只用環保產品和材料來蓋我們房子。

2 形 很嫩的、涉世未深的

My cousin grew up in a small town, so he's still **green** and has a lot to learn about living in the big city.

我表弟在小鎮長大，還很嫩，得多學學怎麼在大城市生存。

green thumb

3 名 擅長園藝者、綠手指

Miranda has a **green thumb**; just look at how beautiful her flower garden is.

米蘭達真是園藝達人，看她美麗的花園就知道了！

　　green 當俚語時可以形容「環保節能的東西」，也可用來描述「天真無知的人」，因為他們就跟植物幼苗一樣嫩。

　　人在種植花草的時候，手指常常被染成綠色，因此，在美國 **green thumb** 用來指「園藝高手」；在英國則是用 green fingers（名詞）或 green-fingered（形容詞）來表達相同意思。

grind [graɪnd]

1 **名 例行公事**

The alarm sounded, and May knew it was time to get up and start the daily **grind**.

鬧鐘響了，梅知道她該起床做每天都要做的事。

2 **名 苦差事、單調無聊的事**

Hanna finds learning Chinese a **grind**.

漢娜覺得學中文是件苦差事。

3 **動 跳舞時以臀部互相廝磨**

Look at those girls **grinding** on the dance floor.

看舞池裡那些扭腰擺臀、互相廝磨的美眉。

on the grind

4 **慣 努力工作**

Todd's been **on the grind**, trying to make enough money to pay his debts.　托德一直很打拼，賺錢還債。

　　已經有工作、要付帳單、房租或貸款的人，會用 **grind** 來表示「每天的例行公事」。

　　單調無聊或很難的事也可以用 grind 來形容，這種事通常都很磨人。

　　在夜店跳舞時，男生、女生常常以屁股磨來磨去、蹭來蹭去，這種扭腰擺臀的跳法，常是為了挑逗對方而跳的，這種動作就可用 grind 來描述。

groove [gruv]

1 名 音樂的節拍

The music had a funky **groove** that made everyone want to get up and dance. 這音樂節拍很強，讓大家都想起來跳舞。

2 動 聽音樂或跟著音樂跳舞

We went to a disco and **grooved** to the music all night long.

我們去舞廳，跟著音樂跳了一整夜。

groovy

3 形 迷人的或時髦的

The models in the magazine always have the **grooviest** outfits on. The clothes must cost a fortune!

雜誌裡的模特兒總穿著最時髦的衣服，那些衣服一定都超貴的！

4 形 好棒的

"Let's go get a beer." "**Groovy!**" 「我們去喝啤酒吧！」「酷斃了！」

get into the groove

5 片 動 回到建立已久的慣例或習慣

It's difficult to **get** back **into the groove** of work after being on holiday for two weeks. 放了兩週假，很難回到工作上。

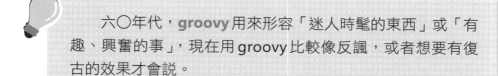

　　六〇年代，**groovy** 用來形容「迷人時髦的東西」或「有趣、興奮的事」，現在用 groovy 比較像反諷，或者想要有復古的效果才會說。

guts [gʌts]

1 名 膽量

The boy was nervous about asking his classmate to dance. After two songs he got up the **guts** to approach her.

男孩一開始不敢開口請同學跳舞，兩首曲子之後，他終於有膽走近她。

He actually had the **guts** to ask me for money again when he didn't even pay me back the last time.

他真敢再跟我開口借錢，上次借的都還沒還呢！

gutsy

2 形 勇敢的

Timmy was quite **gutsy** to defend his friend from those bullies, since they were all much bigger than him.

提米很勇敢，保護朋友免受霸凌，那些人甚至都比他還大隻。

英國人用 gutsy 表示「大膽無畏的」、「意志堅決的」和「勇敢的」，也許這和他們建國以來所經歷的種種戰爭有關，他們需要一個字來形容這些願意為國效命的軍人。今天，gutsy 依然是一個描述性格或行為極佳的形容詞。

hack [hæk]

1 動 駭入他人電腦

My Facebook account must have gotten **hacked**! I didn't write these posts or put up these photos!

我的臉書帳號一定被駭了，我沒發過這些貼文，也沒上傳過這些照片。

2 名 狗仔

In the world of journalism, there are **hacks** and then there are the serious journalists. One should aspire to become the latter.

新聞界有狗仔和正港的記者，大家應該立志成為後者。

3 動 處理

I'm not sure I could **hack** the statistics course.

我不確定我能不能罩得住統計課。

hack into

4 片 動 駭入他人電腦或帳戶

Somebody **hacked into** the bank and transferred a large amount of money from its accounts.

銀行被駭了，帳戶被轉出一大筆錢。

hack up

5 片動 把東西用力咳出來

The patient in the emergency room began **hacking up** blood.
急診室的病人開始咳血。

hack it

6 慣 克服困難而成功

Jill couldn't **hack it** as an artist, so she quit painting and settled for a routine job.
吉兒熬不成藝術家,所以她放棄畫畫,找份安定的工作來做。

　　hack 本來當動詞,表示「砍」、「劈」,它和相關的衍生詞可以代表各種不同的意義,如「狗仔」、「駭」、「處理」、「咳嗽」到「熬出頭」。
　　最常用的應該是「駭」,表示有人非法入侵電腦系統、帳號或銀行帳戶,hacker(駭客)就是指非法入侵者。
　　hack it 常出現在否定句。

hairy [ˈhɛrɪ]

1 形 **恐怖的;危險的**

Walking across the rope bridge was truly a **hairy** experience. I felt as if the bridge would collapse any minute.

過吊橋令人毛骨悚然,我覺得橋隨時會斷。

2 形 **困難重重的**

Steve found the math problems on the college entrance exam to be pretty **hairy**, even though he had studied for weeks.

即使史提夫已經念了好幾個星期,還是覺得大學入學考試的數學題目超難的。

split hairs

3 慣 **不必要的細分**

It makes no difference if we arrive at 2:00 or 2:05, so let's not **split hairs**.

兩點整或是兩點五分到達根本沒差,我們不用這麼錙銖必較。

　　長在你頭上、手上和腿上的「毛髮」(hair),居然能衍生出這些其他的意義,真的很奇妙。

　　hairy 當俚語用時,可以表示「恐怖危險的」或是「困難的」。頭髮已經很細了,再分下去就是給自己找麻煩,**split hairs** 意思就是區分不必要的細節。

068

ham [hæm]

1 **名** 做作的演員

I don't know why audiences think he's a fine actor. He's just an old **ham**.

我不懂為什麼觀眾認為他是個很棒的演員,他明明就很假掰。

ham it up

2 **慣** 誇大其詞

Melody's illness isn't serious. She's just **hamming it up**.

美樂蒂生病又不是很嚴重,她只是愛假仙。

　　ham 原意是「豬肉火腿」,當俚語用時指「做作的演員」和「裝模作樣」。火腿很好吃,但是你可不想成為別人口中的 ham!

　　ham it up 表示說話或是動作刻意很誇張,特別是想搞笑的時候會這樣。

069

039

hammer [`hæmɚ]

1 動 輕易打敗

Eric got **hammered** in the ring by his opponent after only two rounds.　拳擊場上艾瑞克兩回合後就被對手痛宰。

2 動 踩汽車油門

Dustin got into his car and **hammered** down the road to the hospital.　達斯汀一上車就猛踩油門，直奔醫院。

hammered

3 形 喝醉的

Mike and his friends got totally **hammered** at the bar last night.
昨晚在酒吧，麥克和朋友喝得爛醉。

hammer away

4 片 動 致力於某事，直到有成果

The scientists are **hammering away** at finding a cure for this disease.　科學家正絞盡腦汁找出治病的方法。

　　hammer 原指「榔頭」，我們會用榔頭釘釘子，把東西固定好或掛起來。某些俚語用法就是從原意衍生而來的，敲打物品的動作引申為「把對方揍扁」；用力引申為「重踩油門」；東西被敲打後變得扁扁的，引申為「爛醉如泥」。

handle [`hændl]

1 ⑩ 用手摸

Carla is upset because some creepy guy tried to **handle** her when she went up to the bar to get a drink.

卡拉氣死了，她去酒吧喝酒時，有個怪男人想對她毛手毛腳。

2 ⑩ 處理

I don't think I'd be able to **handle** it if Jody ever broke up with me.

如果裘蒂跟我分手，我想我受不了。

3 ⑩ 肢體或言語上保護自己或別人

I wouldn't be worried about Brad getting hurt. He knows how to **handle** himself.

我不擔心布來德會受傷，他懂得怎麼保護自己。

get a handle on

4 ⑩ 了解、掌控情勢或人

We really ought to **get a handle on** the situation before deciding what to do about it.

我們應該先了解情勢，再決定怎麼做。

handle 指的是用手操作，像是用手觸摸或抓握東西，其大多數的俚語用法都跟它的原意密切相關，因為它們描述的都是抓著某人或某物的動作，並和你的手或手部動作有關。

040

hang up one's hat

1 慣 退休

After having worked for more than 30 years as a detective, Brian decided to hang up his hat and retire to the country.

當了 30 幾年的警探，布萊恩打算高掛警帽，退休到鄉下養老。

hang-up [ˋhæŋ͵ʌp]

2 名 （精神或感情上的）煩惱，焦慮；困難，問題

Lora has so many emotional hang-ups. She should really talk to someone about her problems.

蘿拉有很多情緒問題，她真該找人談談的。

hung up

3 形 被耽擱的

Sorry I'm late. I got hung up in traffic.

對不起，我遲到了，被交通給耽擱了。

4 形 緊張焦慮的

Sally is always hung up about the way she looks. I told her she should be more confident.

莎莉總是很緊張自己的外表，我叫她要有自信一點。

5 形 因往事心情受影響

Don't get too **hung up** over your relationship with Carl.
He's really not worth it.

不要因為卡爾心情不好，他根本不值得你這樣。

hung up on

6 慣 念念不忘的

Hanna doesn't want to get into a new relationship yet because
she's still **hung up on** her ex-boyfriend.

漢娜還不想開始新戀情，因為她念念不忘前男友。

　　hang本意為「懸掛」、「安裝」。男生下班一進家門，就
會把帽子脫掉，掛在架子上；這個動作引申為「退休」，當人
想要永遠離開工作崗位，就可以用 hang up one's hat 來表
達。

　　hang-up 指精神或感情上的煩惱、焦慮或困難、問題，
不是好事。

　　如果你變得 hung up on，就表示你對某事或某人「念念
不忘」。

hard-core [ˈhɑrdˌkor]

1

形 純正的；正宗的

When I was growing up, I loved listening to **hard-core** heavy metal.

我青少年時期，愛聽正宗重金屬搖滾樂。

2

形 十足的罪犯或徹底不正常之人

Alcatraz was a prison for **hard-core** criminals.

惡魔島監獄專關窮凶惡極的罪犯。

3

形 （A片）真槍實彈的、赤裸裸的

The actor made some sexy movies at the start of his career, but he was never involved in any **hard-core** porn.

那演員剛入行時拍了一些情色電影，但沒拍過真槍實彈的 A 片。

4

形 瘋狂喜歡某人或做某件事

Melissa is **hard-core** about working out. She wakes up every morning at 5 AM and goes to the gym.

瑪麗莎非常熱中於健身，她每天早上五點起床去健身房健身。

　　東西很 hard，表示它不易穿透、質地堅硬，**hard-core** 描述的正是這些特質，但是在程度上更為嚴重，最常用來指「正宗的」、「窮凶惡極的重刑犯」、「不正常的性行為」，或是「瘋狂喜愛某事」。可以把 hard-core 當作形容詞，用來描述任何你想描述的事物，從 a hard-core movie buff（死忠影迷）到 a hard-core stamp collector（集郵狂），或是其他種種的「……狂」。

hassle [`hæs!]

1 動 煩擾、打擾

There's no need for you to drive me to the airport. I don't want to **hassle** you.

你不用載我去機場，我不想麻煩你。

2 動 騷擾

African-Americans often get **hassled** by the police even when they've done nothing wrong.

就算沒犯錯，非裔美國人也經常被警察騷擾。

3 名 麻煩、難題

I had my purse stolen while I was on holiday, so I had to go through the **hassle** of going to the police station and calling my bank to put a block on my credit card.

度假時，我錢包被偷，我得處理一堆麻煩事，跑警局，打電話掛失信用卡。

　　hassle 的原意和俚語用法是可以互換的，不管你指的是原意或俚語用法，你都不想被 hassle。hassle 是一種「騷擾」，也就是不斷地被「激怒」或「煩擾」。

head trip ['hɛd,trɪp]

1

名 自我妄想

Sarah is on such a **head trip**. She thinks everyone in the world worships her.

莎拉又在妄想了，她以為世上每個人都崇拜她。

2

名 服用迷幻藥後產生的妄想

He used to drop acid and go on these **head trips** that would last for days.

他以前嗑藥，都會妄想個好幾天。

3

名 思想神遊

The book was a total **head trip** into the feelings and thoughts of a serial killer.

這本書讓人一窺究竟連續殺人魔的內心世界。

head trip 望文生義就是「思想的旅行」。你不需走出家門，就可以進行這趟旅程！

它可以是趟小小的旅行，讓你好好思考自己的行為，但是你還是不應太常 head trip，否則你腦袋裡可能會產生「妄想」。

head trip 也指「喝醉或吸毒之後所產生的妄想」。

heavy [ˈhɛvɪ]

1 形 繁重的

With Charlotte's **heavy** workload, she didn't know if she could hack going back to school part time.

夏綠蒂的工作繁重，她實在不知道自己有沒有辦法同時兼顧回學校上課。

2 形 使用或準備使用暴力的

The bouncers usually try to stop fights before they start, but sometimes they have to get **heavy** and throw people out of the club.

保鑣通常在鬥毆發生前就阻止人開打，不過，有時他們也得使用暴力，把人扔出舞廳。

3 形 覺得有壓力的

Things between Ian and Lisa got **heavy**, so the two of them decided to take a break from each other and see other people.

伊恩和麗莎兩人之間越來越不開心，所以他們決定分開，跟其他人約會。

heavy 是形容詞，指「沉重的」、「費力的」或是「超越一般的」。它最常用的俚語用法便集結了這所有的特質。

如果有東西困擾你，增加了你的負擔，讓你的生活更難過，而且這些狀況通常比一般的問題更嚴重，你就可以說 Now that is heavy!。

hit [hɪt]

1 名 吸一口大麻

Someone passed him a joint, so he took a **hit**.

有人給他一根大麻，他哈了一口。

2 動 喝很多酒

Every night after work, Jeremy would **hit** the bottle. His friends told him that he had a drinking problem and needed help, but he wouldn't listen.

每晚下班傑瑞米都喝很多酒，朋友跟他說他有酗酒問題，需要專業協助，但他聽不進去。

3 名 暗殺或謀殺

Tom's death wasn't the result of an accident but rather a professional **hit**.

湯姆不是死於意外，而是職業殺手幹的。

4 動 為顧客倒飲料

Hey, bartender, **hit** me again. This time make it a double!

嘿，老兄，再給我酒，這次給我雙份的。

5 名 點擊次數

Linda's blog receives thousands of **hits** each day.

琳達的部落格每天都有數以千計的點擊次數。

6 名 成功且受歡迎的人或物

The clown that Jessica hired for her son's birthday turned out to be a real **hit** with all the kids.

潔西卡為兒子舉辦生日趴，請了一個小丑，結果超受孩子喜愛。

　　用 **hit** 表示「為顧客倒飲料」源於美國；現在 hit 最常見的用法應該就是指網站或影片的「點擊率」，就是造訪人次。

horn [hɔrn]

1 名 電話

"I need to speak with Jake. Get him on the horn right now!" Tom said to his secretary.

湯姆跟秘書說：「我要跟傑克說話，馬上打電話給他。」

horny

2 形 性興奮的

After a few drinks Eddie gets really horny.

喝了幾杯酒後，艾迪色性大發。

3 形 好色的

The bar was full of horny guys trying to get lucky.

酒吧裡全是一些色鬼，想找人上床。

這是一個很好玩的字，horn 原指有蹄動物頭上的「角」，以及「喇叭」，當俚語時，指「電話」。
horny 則是形容老想跟別人上床的人。

hot [hɑt]

1 形 極好的、很棒的；很紅的

The new smartphones that have come out this year are really **hot**. They're top of the line and their designs are state-of-the-art.

今年新上市的智慧手機真是讚，品質佳，設計新潮。

2 形 性感的

I met this really **hot** girl at the pub yesterday, and she actually gave me her phone number.

昨晚我在夜店遇到這個超辣的美眉，她真的留電話給我。

3 形 以非法方式獲得的

The electronics this guy is selling are **hot**. Why else do you think he's letting them go for so cheap?

這傢伙賣的電子產品都是非法得來的，不然你以為為什麼這麼便宜。

4 形 危險的

The police officer called for backup because he saw that the situation might get too **hot** for him to handle alone.

因為情勢越來越危險，警官一個人無法掌控，所以他趕快請求支援。

hot zone

5 名 危險地區

Right now in the Middle East, soldiers are constantly living and working in **hot zones**. No one is really safe!

此刻位於中東的士兵分分秒秒都在衝突一觸即發的地區生活與工作，沒有人是安全的！

　　hot當俚語時，意義有正面的，也有負面的；正面用法的hot可形容某物很夯、很讚，也可以形容人很辣；負面意味的hot可指「非法取得」，有些電視、DVD或音響因為是贓物，所以特別便宜；情勢緊張、危險時，也可以用hot形容。

　　hot zone是指「危險地帶」，這些地區因為生化、核武、病毒或暴力的關係，極度危險，必須以特殊設備保護當地居民，因為他們很可能會染病或被迫害。如果你在新聞中看到關於非洲伊波拉病毒和中東戰爭的報導，就會聽到記者或主播用hot zone來形容這些情勢危險的地區。

044

hump [hʌmp]

1

動 背、扛、舉起

The elevator was broken, so we had to **hump** our suitcases up the stairs to our apartment.

電梯壞掉了，所以我們得爬樓梯，把行李箱扛到公寓。

2

動 性交；做愛

Chris's dog has the habit of **humping** people's legs.

克里斯的狗常把人的腳當母狗來上。

hump day

3

名 星期三

Everyone loves Wednesday because it's **hump day**. The weekend is almost here and the workweek is almost over!

每個人都喜歡星期三，因為星期三算是小週末。一到這天，就表示週末快到，上班的日子就快結束了！

在軍中，**hump** 表示「背」或「扛」東西，這種說法持續至今天，但多是那些穿著制服的軍人在使用。如果你在 hump something，這個東西通常很重，甚至重達你體重的一半，當你 hump 軍備時通常在險惡的狀況下，此時你往往得背著東西走上好幾天、好幾星期，為的就是找到敵人。

hump day 通常用來指週三，星期三是一週的中間，星期一、二時就好像在爬山丘（hump），星期三爬上山頂，所以可以祝人 Happy Hump Day（小週末快樂），因為一星期已經過了一半，再過兩天就要放假了。

icky ['ɪki]

1 形 沒品味的

Others may consider these photos to be art, but I find them **icky** and disturbing to look at.

別人也許認為這些照片是藝術，但我覺得它們很低俗，而且很傷眼。

2 形 討厭的、味道不好的、黏黏的

What you're eating might taste good, but it certainly looks **icky**.

你吃的東西也許很美味，但是看起來很噁爛。

3 形 甜得發膩的、老套的

Not being a very sentimental person, Keira found the love letter that Bill had written to her to be somewhat **icky**.

奇拉並不是個多情的人，比爾寫給她的情書讓她覺得肉麻。

只要聽過一次 **icky**，你就能猜出它的意義，它用來形容「沒品味的東西」、「令人討厭的事物」或「令人倒胃口的東西」。

081

046

jack [dʒæk]

1 動 搶劫

I can't believe my bike got **jacked**. I left it outside the store just a few minutes ago.

我不敢相信我腳踏車被搶了，我只不過停在店家外面幾分鐘而已。

2 名 什麼也不懂

Stop acting like you know what you're talking about. You don't know **jack**!

別再擺出那副自以為什麼都知道的樣子，你根本什麼都不懂！

3 形 壯的

Man, that guy looks **jacked**! He must work out every day.

靠！那男的看起來好壯，他一定每天健身。

　　在美國，**jack** 有兩種用法，都相當常見：一是「被搶劫」，這個用法源於大城市，像是紐約或洛杉機；二是「什麼也沒有（nothing）」，如果你對某事一無所知，就可以說：

I don't know jack about it! 我什麼都不知道！

這句話也就是指I don't know anything about it.。jack常常和動詞know一起出現。

jack off

1 片動 打手槍

He **jacked off**, looking at a picture of a naked woman in a magazine.

他看著雜誌裡裸女的照片打手槍。

2 形 惱怒、生氣

I was so **jacked off** when I missed the train to Taipei.

我錯過去台北的火車，氣得要命。

3 名 蠢蛋

Christopher was acting like a **jack off**, so no one wanted to hang out with him.

克里斯多夫像個豬頭，沒人想跟他一塊出去。

jack up

4 片動 興奮或激動

Corrine was really **jacked up** about going to Hong Kong this weekend; she couldn't wait to go shopping.

寇琳這週末要去香港，興奮得不得了，她等不及要去大血拼了。

jack off 最常用來表示「手淫」；第二常見的就是表示「生氣」，事實上，如果有人激怒你或不理你，你可能就會罵對方 jack off（蠢蛋）。

047 ▶

jam [dʒæm]

1 名 陷入困境

Stephanie is stuck in a **jam**. She made dinner plans with her husband to celebrate their first anniversary, but now her boss wants her to stay in the office to finish a report.

史黛芬妮陷入兩難，她計畫跟老公共進晚餐，慶祝第一個結婚紀念日，但是老闆要她留在辦公室完成報告。

2 名 塞車

Sorry I'm late. I got held up in a **jam** on the highway.

抱歉，我遲到了，在高速公路上塞車。

3 動 與其他音樂家即興表演

Eddie plays the guitar, and he was really excited to have a chance to **jam** with his favorite jazz band.

艾迪會彈吉他，有機會跟他最愛的爵士樂團即興表演讓他很興奮。

4 名 即興演奏的歌曲

I like this coffee shop because it always has cool **jams** playing on the stereo.

我很喜歡這間咖啡店，因為它會播放超酷的即興樂曲。

jam 源於美國，成年人之間最常用 jam 表示「陷入某種困境」，被卡住的意思。

jam 還可以指即興演奏，比如爵士樂手常常在樂曲中穿插一段即興表演。This is my favorite jam. 意思是這是我（最愛）的歌。

jazz up [ˋdʒæzˌʌp]

1 片動 裝飾

Simon **jazzed up** his dull-looking apartment with some pictures and a colorful rug.

賽門用幾幅畫和鮮豔的地毯裝點他那了無生氣的公寓。

2 片動 賦予生氣

The crowds were really **jazzed up** as the marching band passed by.

遊行樂隊經過時，人群更加興奮了。

jazzy

3 形 花俏的

I'm not looking for anything **jazzy**. I just want a simple, black dress that's appropriate for a business dinner.

我不要太花俏的，只要簡單、黑色的洋裝，可以得體出席商務晚餐就好。

　　jazz 原本指「爵士樂」，是一種美式音樂，當俚語用可指「裝飾」、「賦予生氣」、「花俏的」。

jerk [dʒɝk]

1 名 傻瓜

He has been acting like a **jerk** lately. I have no idea what has gotten into him.

他最近豬頭豬腦的，不知道他怎麼了。

jerk around

2 片動 激怒

The store clerk wouldn't let me return the shirt even though the tag was still on it and I had the receipt. I told her to stop **jerking** me **around** and to let me speak to her manager.

標籤還在衣服上面，收據也還在，店員竟然不肯讓我退貨，我叫她不要再惹我，叫她的經理出來跟我說。

3 片動 侮辱

Aaron is always breaking dates with Mindy. If he doesn't stop **jerking** her **around**, she's going to break up with him.

艾倫約會老是放明蒂鴿子，如果他再這樣侮辱她，她就要跟他分手！

jerk off

4 名 討厭的男人

Ryan got drunk at the party and started acting like a **jerk off**. The next morning, he couldn't remember anything.

雷恩在派對喝醉，開始像個混球，隔天卻什麼也記不得。

5 片 動 打手槍

Marc **jerked off** while he drove his car home from work the other night.

馬克前幾天晚上下班開車回家時，在車上打手槍。

　　以上幾種說法有很多種意思，它們大多都由jerk衍生而來，意義也都相當類似。其中兩個定義源自美國：一是**jerk someone around**，表示激怒他人，二是**jerk off**，指討厭的男人。

　　無論是什麼意思，你都不想當那個被jerked around（激怒或侮辱）的人，也不想當jerk someone around的人，這是不對的行為，而且會讓對方看起來像個 jerk（傻瓜）。視情況不同，你自己也可能會被別人視為 jerk off（討厭的男人）！

John Doe

1 名 無名男屍；無名男性

We have a **John Doe**, late forties. He died of carbon monoxide poisoning. 我們有具無名男屍，年近五十，死於一氧化碳中毒。

Jane Doe

2 名 無名女屍；無名女性

The police officers are hopeful that they'll soon be able to identify **Jane Doe**. 警察有信心很快就能查出無名女屍的身分了。

John Hancock

3 名 親筆簽名

Put your **John Hancock** right here on the bottom of the contract and the house is yours.

請在合約下方簽名，這間房子就是你的了！

　　John Doe 和 **Jane Doe** 用於美國和加拿大，原是法庭給不知姓名當事人的假稱，後來指「無名屍」，男的叫John Doe，女的叫Jane Doe。在醫院，失去意識、身分不明的病人，也被這麼稱呼。英國、澳洲和紐西蘭則用Joe Bloggs或John Smith指相同事物。

　　John Hancock（約翰‧漢考克）是美國政治家、革命家，也是一名富商，1776年美國簽署獨立宣言時，他是第一個簽名的人，由於他的親筆簽名非常華麗，之後他的名字也成了親筆簽名的代稱。

juice [dʒus]

1 名 油或電

My car broke down and needed to be jumped. When the cables were connected to the engine, the mechanic told me to start the engine and give it some **juice**.

我的車壞了，得送修，引擎接上電線後，技師叫我發動，給車子送電。

2 名 八卦、勁爆新聞

This magazine contains all the latest **juice** on your favorite Hollywood stars.

這雜誌蒐集了你最愛的好萊塢影星的最新八卦。

3 名 酒

The woman who lived on the seventh floor always had **juice** in her hand. It would be in her coffee in the morning, in her tea at lunch, and then in her tonic water in the evening.

住七樓那女的老是酒不離手，她早上的咖啡、中午的茶、晚上的汽水都加了酒。

juiced

4 形 喝醉的

Boy, that guy was **juiced**! He stumbled out of the club and could hardly stand up straight when he was hailing a taxi.

哇，那個男的真的醉了！他搖搖晃晃地走出夜店，連叫計程車都站不穩。

juice up

5 片動 賦予生氣

We need to **juice up** this place; it's supposed to be a party and no one is dancing!

我們來讓這裡熱鬧一點吧，這應該是個派對耶，卻沒有人在跳舞！

juicy

6 形 性感誘人的

The rapper rapped about women's butts being big, round, and **juicy**.

這饒舌歌手唱饒舌歌，說唱女生屁股又大、又圓又性感。

juice 原指「果汁」，「酒」和「喝醉的」的俚語用法與原意有關。

說到車子，像是踩油門加速的時候，常常會說：「Give it some juice.（給它一點動力。）」。

juicy 也出現在饒舌歌裡，而且多是形容「性感的臀部」，像是 She is big, round, and juicy.（她屁股又大又圓又性感。），你出去玩時可能會聽到這樣的句子，而且一定是出自男性口中。不過這樣的說法最好別隨便亂用。

junkie [ˈdʒʌŋkɪ]

1

名 愛吃垃圾食物的人

So many kids today are junk-food **junkies**. At school, they hardly eat any fruit or veggies for lunch.

很多孩子都愛吃垃圾食物，學校午餐幾乎不吃水果或蔬菜。

2

名 毒蟲

It was only a year ago that he tried heroin for the first time, and today, he's become a **junkie**.

一年前他才第一次吸海洛因，現在已經變毒蟲了。

　　junkie 最常用來指「毒蟲」，不過，只要是對某個東西上癮的人（食物、酒精、毒品、漫畫、香菸等），我們都可以稱之為 junkie，這個字適用於所有能讓你「一陣興奮」的事物。
　　但如果你只是對漫畫、電影或書上癮，junkie 就沒有負面意了。身為 junkie 並不一定都不好，看你是對什麼上癮。

089

keep . . . (emotions)

keep a stiff upper lip

1 慣 不灰心、不氣餒

Damian wasn't chosen for the medical internship, but he **kept a stiff upper lip**. He worked hard for this and was determined to try again next semester.

達米安沒選上實習醫師，但是他咬緊牙關，努力打拼，決心下學期再來一次！

keep a straight face

2 慣 憋笑

When Albert sang and danced for my birthday, I tried so hard to **keep a straight face**. I almost peed my pants for how funny it was!

艾伯特在我生日那天又唱又跳，我努力憋住不笑，實在太爆笑了，我差點笑到尿褲子了。

keep one's cool

3 慣 保持冷靜

When Samuel asked Isabella to marry him, he was afraid he wouldn't be able to **keep his cool** and that he would mess up the marriage proposal.

山繆要跟伊莎貝拉求婚時，他擔心自己太緊張，沒辦法冷靜，會把求婚搞砸。

keep on keeping on

4 慣 堅持不懈

Tina and Steven had been dating for over five years. When they broke up, Tina knew she'd have to **keep on keeping on** if she was going to get through this tough time.

蒂娜和史提芬已經在一起五年多了，他們分手時，蒂娜知道她要不斷努力才能熬過這段痛苦期。

這些俚語現今還是廣泛使用，它們有一個共通點，就是在經歷情緒轉變時才會使用，通常是難過、沮喪、不幸，或是無法控制的事情發生時。

keep . . . (information)

keep an eye on

1 慣 照看；注意

Please **keep an eye on** the child. He gets into mischief easily.

請看著那個孩子，他很容易調皮搗蛋。

keep one's ear to the ground

2 慣 注意聽

When you are new in town, you should always **keep your ear to the ground** but keep your mouth closed. You'll be much better off that way.

剛到一個地方，你最好多聽少說，這樣會比較順利。

keep tabs on

3 慣 保持最新資訊

Now that Margo lives in Taiwan, she often goes on Facebook to **keep tabs on** what her friends back in the States are up to.

瑪歌現在住台灣，她常上臉書，看以前美國的朋友在幹嘛。

以上幾個用法都是「獲得資訊」，有趣的是，其中兩個說法還跟身體部位有關：**keep an eye on** 和 **keep one's ear to the ground**，兩種獲取資訊的作法，這幾個都是流通世界各地的片語。

key [ki]

1 名 根本

The **key** to the problem is communication! Always talk things out immediately and never go to bed angry.

問題的根本是「溝通」！一定要隨時把內心話講出來，不要帶著悶氣去睡覺。

2 名 一公斤毒品

The man tried to get past customs inspection with two **keys** of coke strapped to his body.

那男的身上綁了兩公斤古柯鹼，試圖通過海關檢查。

　　如果你沒有 **key**，就開不了鎖，了解 key 的原意，它的俚語意義「根本」也就不難記了。

　　key 也可以用來指「一公斤毒品」，跟公斤（kilo）的音有關，毒蟲和毒販最常用這個字。

kick [kɪk]

1 名 便鞋或運動鞋

Kevin bought a new pair of **kicks** to wear to school every day.

凱文買了一雙每天要穿去上學的新便鞋。

2 名 刺激

We went to the first party, had some **kicks**, then left and went to the second party.

我們先去一個派對找點刺激,然後又跑去別的派對玩。

3 名 樂子

He gets his **kicks** out of reading mystery novels.

他讀神秘小說找樂子。

I sing for **kicks**, but I'm not really good at it.

我唱歌唱好玩的,我實在不太會唱。

> **kick** 原意是「踢」,當俚語時,kick 表示「輕鬆方便的鞋子或運動鞋」,源於美國黑人圈。
> kick 還可表示「刺激」或「快樂的事」。

kick around

1 片動 輕鬆地討論

I have some ideas for the marketing campaign that I'd like to **kick around** with the rest of the team.

關於行銷策略,我想到一些點子,想跟隊友討論一下。

2 片動 漫無目的地亂晃

On the weekends we just get on our scooters and **kick around**. We never know where we'll end up!

週末,我們就騎機車到處亂晃,從來不知道目的地在哪!

這是一個常聽到的俚語,你可以 **kick around**(隨興講講)一些想法或建議。

kick around 也可表示「沒有目的地亂晃」。

kick ass

1 名 了不起的人

Will thought he was such a **kick ass** when it came to fighting.

講到打架，威爾覺得自己真的很厲害。

2 慣 以強硬的方式展現自己的能力

The coach told his team "Now get out on the field and **kick some ass**!"

教練告訴他的隊員：「上場，讓對方好看。」

3 慣 表現很好

I **kicked ass** on that exam!

我考得超棒的！

4 形 玩得開心

That trip we took to the beach today was **kick ass**. I had such a good time.

我們今天去海邊真是超好玩的，我玩得超開心。

kick somebody's ass

5 片動 教訓人，讓對方受傷

If he says anything disrespectful to you, let me know and I'll **kick his ass**.

如果他對你說話不客氣，告訴我，我給他點顏色瞧瞧。

6 片動 打敗某人

Bill **kicked Jona's ass** in the tennis match.

比爾在網球比賽中打敗喬娜。

在美國，**kick ass** 表示「麻煩人物」或「以強硬的方式展現自己的能力」，但 kick ass 還可用來表示「表現很棒」或是「玩得開心」。

kick someone's ass 很常用來表示「教訓對方」或「打敗對方」，是很生動的說法。

kickback

1 名 賄賂

The city officials received a **kickback** for every contract it granted to private firms.

市政官員發包給私人企業時都會收賄。

kick back

2 片 動 放鬆

Tonight, all I want to do is **kick back** with my boyfriend and just enjoy each other's company.

我今天晚上只想跟男友好好放鬆一下，享受彼此的陪伴。

kick in

3 片 動 開始作用

Tommy took his cold medicine around 8 PM, but he was still waiting for it to **kick in** an hour later.

湯米大概晚上八點吃了感冒藥，但一小時後他還在等藥發揮效用。

kick it

4 慣 死

The goldfish that Johnny won at the fair Saturday afternoon **kicked it** by Sunday morning.

強尼星期六下午在遊園會贏到的金魚，星期天早上就死翹翹了。

5 慣 放鬆；晃一下

I'm just going to **kick it** for a few minutes. Then, I'll get back to work.

我去晃一下再回來工作。

kick someone or something to the curb

6 慣 拒絕

After all of his childish antics, Lisa **kicked him to the curb**. She couldn't date a guy who acted like that.

因為他舉止幼稚可笑，麗莎把他甩了，她無法跟這種男生交往。

    kickback 和 **kick back** 都源於美國，工作太忙的時候，你只想要 kick back（放鬆）一下。

    kick it（死亡）不常用來描述人，多用來描述動物，像是寵物鼠、金魚或狗。

    kick someone/something to the curb 也是美式用法，它最常用在當你不再喜歡對方，想要甩掉對方的時候。

kick off ['kɪk,ɔf]

1 片動 生氣，打起架來

Oscar and Patrick were talking calmly to each other, and then they suddenly **kicked off** at each other without any seeming reason.

奧斯卡和派翠克原本平靜地談話，後來兩人莫名其妙打起架來。

2 片動 比賽開始

The game is about to **kick off**. Let's go to our seats.

比賽要開打了，趕快去我們的位子坐吧！

3 片動 死

I just found out that the old woman who lived next door to me **kicked off** in her sleep two nights ago. It was a very peaceful way to go.

我剛剛才知道隔壁老太太兩天前在睡夢中去世，走得很安詳。

4 片動 離開

The boat **kicked off** from the port at noon on Sunday.

那艘船星期天中午離港了。

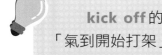

　　kick off 的幾個用法都源於美國，其中最常見的用法是「氣到開始打架」，它也可以用來表示「運動比賽開始」，運動比賽多指美式足球。

　　至於用 kick off 表示「死亡、去世」多是老一輩在用。近來比較少用 kick off 表「離開」，現在較常用 shove off 和 bounce。

kicker [ˈkɪkɚ]

1 名 令人驚訝事情發生變化

Janice never plays the lottery, but she decided to buy a ticket this time. The **kicker** is that she actually won the jackpot!

珍妮斯沒買過彩券，但這次她決定買一張，妙的是她真的中頭獎了！

2 名 不利的潛在因素，常指合約裡的條文

My father always told me to read contracts carefully for **kickers** that may end up being a problem for me. I've learned to read everything, even the fine print, before putting down my John Hancock.

我爸總是提醒我要詳閱合約內容，特別是那些可能讓我惹上麻煩的條文，簽名前，我已學會什麼都檢查，連小字印刷的附屬細則也不放過。

　　kicker 的兩種俚語用法都源於美國，也都很常用。讓你驚訝的事，可用 kicker 描述。

　　每次要簽合約或是重要的文件前，記得要看看裡面有沒有什麼問題，有些附屬細則的字體比正文還小，很容易忽略，有時不利的條文（kicker）就在那堆小字裡。

kill [kɪl]

1 動 吃完、喝光

He was so hungry when he came back from rugby practice that he **killed** everything in the refrigerator.

他練完英式橄欖球回來後，餓到把冰箱裡的東西都吃光了。

2 動 終止

Everyone was disappointed when the boss decided to **kill** the project because they had all worked so hard on it.

老闆決定終止計畫案時，大家都很失落，因為他們努力了很久。

kill the noise

3 慣 不出聲、把音樂關掉

I need you to **kill the noise** so I can explain the rules of the game.

我拜託你別再吵，這樣我才可以解釋比賽規則。

Adam screamed, "**Kill the noise**, or I'm going to throw your stereo out the window!"

亞當大喊：「把音樂關掉，不然我就把你的音響從窗戶丟出去！」

以上的用法都很有趣。如果你 **kill something**，則表示你把某個東西吃完或把某事做完了，像是書本、雜誌、電玩，甚至是你的回家作業。

kill the noise 源於美國，當你很生氣，想「把音樂、電視關掉」或是「叫對方閉嘴」，就可以用。

killer ['kɪlɚ]

1 ⑱ 非常時髦的

The clothes that the women in Hollywood wear are **killer**! They can afford all the latest trends.

好萊塢女星都穿得很時髦，她們買得起最新的行頭。

2 ⑲ 非常困難

Ralph said that the GMAT was a **killer**, and he's not sure if he did well on it.

瑞夫說 GMAT 真的超難的，他不確定他考得怎樣。

3 ⑱ 很好的、很棒的

Did you see Jim catch that **killer** wave? That was awesome!

你有沒有看到吉姆衝到那個超級大浪？真是太讚了！

4 ⑱ 很濃的、很強的

Rory always sold **killer** bud. It was very expensive though.

羅瑞老是在賣很強的大麻，不過也很貴就是了。

　　killer 的俚語用法變化多端，最常用的意義是「時髦的服裝」、「最新的電影」、「流行的書籍」等任何最時髦最流行的事物。雖然這個字已經不像以前使用得那麼普遍，你還是可以常常聽到。衝浪迷喜歡用 killer 談論他們衝過的超級大浪。

knacker [`nækə]

1 名 睪丸

In Europe, some men might wear tight swim shorts at the beach to show off their **knackers**.

在歐洲有些男的喜歡在海邊穿緊身泳褲，炫耀他們的蛋蛋。

2 名 小人

That fucking **knacker** stole my car!

那混蛋偷了我的車。

knackering

3 形 使疲倦的、使筋疲力竭的

What a **knackering** week I had! It was nonstop work every day.

這週真是太操了，我每天工作個不停。

knackered

4 形 筋疲力盡的

Chris looks totally **knackered**. What has he been doing to make him look so tired?

克里斯看起來累趴了，他幹啥了這麼累啊？

你最常聽到 **knackered** 的時間，多是深夜或是狂歡了一晚後的早上，每個人都精疲力竭，睡到下午才醒來喝下午茶！

knockoff [ˈnɑkˌɔf]

1 名 **複製品或仿品**

The painting is a **knockoff** of the original one at the museum.
那幅畫是博物館原作的複製品。

knock off

2 片動 **搶劫或偷取**

The crooks were professionals; they only **knocked off** the real jewels and not the copies that are displayed in case of robberies.
這群小偷是專家，他們只偷真的珠寶，不偷防搶用的仿造展示珠寶。

3 片動 **殺死**

In the movie, the heroine **knocks off** three people.
電影裡的女主角殺了三個人。

4 片動 **停工、停止**

In the summer, Vincent likes to **knock off** work a few hours earlier. 夏天的時候，文森喜歡提早幾個鐘頭下班。

Please **knock off** what you are doing. It disrupts the class.
住手！你這樣打斷大家上課了。

 很多小偷會偷名畫和珠寶，有時他們不知道偷的只是 **knockoff**（複製品）；有些賊把贗品和真品對調，這樣就沒人發現東西被偷了。

在美國，被黑幫 **knocked off**（殺死）是常發生的事。

L

lash [læʃ]

1 動 嘗試

Mary didn't want to think of herself as a quitter. She had to **lash** at least one more time to hit the ball.

瑪莉不想當一個輕易放棄的人，決定再試一次，看能不能打到球。

go on the lash

2 名 喝酒狂歡

All the seniors were so excited to have finally graduated high school. They **went on the lash**.

終於畢業了，所有的高三學生都興奮得不得了，跑去狂歡。

lash down

3 片 動 下大雨

We didn't go out all afternoon because the rain has been **lashing down** nonstop.

我們整個下午都沒出門，因為大雨下個不停。

lash out

片 動 突然對某人言語攻擊

Ryan was upset with Sam and **lashed out** at him.

雷恩氣山姆氣得對他破口大罵。

lash在不同地區有不同意思。在澳洲、紐西蘭用lash表「嘗試」，也會以 have a lash at something 的形式出現！

在英國，**be/go on the lash** 是指「喝酒狂歡」。**lash down** 指下大雨，像用倒的那種豪雨。

lash最普遍、通行各英語國家的用法就是 **lash out**，源於美國，形容人「破口大罵」。

lay [le]

1 名 性交

He's just interested in you for a quick **lay**. Don't be taken in by his charms.

他只想趕快跟你上床，不要被他的花言巧語騙了。

2 名 上床對象

I took Sandra home last night. Yeah, she was a good **lay**.

我昨晚帶珊卓回家了，沒錯，她真是上床咖。

get laid

3 慣 做愛；上床

Brad hasn't **gotten laid** in over a month.

布萊德已超過一個月沒嘿咻了。

想要 **get laid** 或是 **have a lay** 的人很多，常被隨意說出口，但它並非用來描述「性交」最好聽的字。

且身為一個 lay（上床對象）不是一件光榮的事。

lay back

1 慣 放鬆的

Just **lay back** and enjoy the ride. I will take care of everything.

你就放輕鬆好好享受兜風的快感,其他的事就交給我吧!

2 形 隨和的

Tiffany is so **laid-back**. She never gets upset about anything.

蒂芬妮總是很隨和,從來不發脾氣。

lay down

3 片 動 放棄戰鬥

After weeks of fighting, the soldiers finally **laid down** their weapons and surrendered to their enemy.

打了幾個禮拜以後,士兵終於放下武器向敵軍投降。

lay back 最常用於北美洲,每個人都想要 lay back,輕輕鬆鬆的,不必擔心任何事。

lay down 表示兩方同意不再打仗,但不一定是投降。

059 ▶

lay one on someone

1 慣 打、揍

If Mattie tries to date my little sister, I will **lay one on him**.

要是麥堤想把我妹，我會揍他一頓。

lay out

2 片動 被揍扁

Martin got **laid out** by a gang while jogging in the park.

馬丁在公園慢跑時被幫派分子海扁一頓。

　　這兩個俚語都跟打架有關，不過，如果這些事發生在你身上，那就不好玩了！其中 **lay one on someone** 較常用，這代表你使用暴力。

　　如果有人打架被對方打昏了，那你也可以説：「They got **laid out.**」。這種事通常發生在深夜酒吧外面。

leery ['lɪri]

1 形 防衛心重的

Having grown up in New York, Amber has always been **leery** around strangers. 從小在紐約長大，安柏在陌生人面前防衛心很重。

2 形 小心的、謹慎的

I'm not saying you shouldn't stay at that hotel. Just be **leery**. It isn't the best in the neighborhood.

我不是說你不應該住旅館，我只希望你小心一點，因為那一帶並不是非常安全。

3 形 脾氣不好的

Amelia was very **leery**. The tiniest thing would set her off and she would lash out at whoever made her mad.

艾蜜莉亞脾氣很差，芝麻小事都會惹到她，她就會把對方罵得狗血淋頭。

4 形 靠不住的、不可信的

I would stay away from that bloke. He appears to be a bit **leery**!

我會離那個傢伙遠一點，他是個不可靠的人！

leery 這幾種用法中有兩個源於英國，其中只有一個橫越大西洋，傳到北美。用 leery 表示「脾氣不好的」仍只限於英國，不過，用 leery 表示「不可信賴的」則使用於世界各地，哪裡有 leery 的人，你就可以在哪裡使用這個字！

leery 使用於北美時，多用來提醒對方提防某人，也許那些人不肯相信別人或是脾氣不好，但是通常是因為那些人不可靠。

lemon [ˈlɛmən]

1
名 傻瓜、出糗的人

Jeffrey fell down the stairs in school before lunch. He felt like such a **lemon** because Julie, the girl he likes, saw him.

傑弗瑞午餐前在學校跌下樓梯，他覺得好糗，因為被他喜歡的女生茱莉看到了。

2
名 沒用的人、爛東西

The first car that Susan ever bought was a **lemon**. She didn't know a thing about cars and she went to an unreliable car dealer.

蘇珊買的第一輛車真是廢鐵，她對車一竅不通，又跑去跟一個不可靠的車商買車。

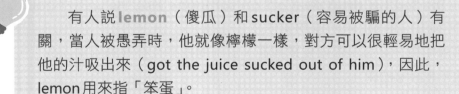
有人說 lemon（傻瓜）和 sucker（容易被騙的人）有關，當人被愚弄時，他就像檸檬一樣，對方可以很輕易地把他的汁吸出來（got the juice sucked out of him），因此，lemon 用來指「笨蛋」。

檸檬外表很漂亮，但吃起來味道卻酸酸的，與負面情緒產生關聯，所以 lemon 被用來指「沒用、讓你不滿意的東西」，生活、爛車都可以用 lemon 來形容。

load [lod]

1 名 個人需要的毒品量

James went to pick up his **load** from the guy on the corner. He doesn't even know his name. He just gets his supply and goes.

詹姆斯跑去街角跟那男的補貨，他根本不知道對方的名字，只拿了貨就走了。

shoot one's load

2 慣 射精

The boy got so excited looking at the dirty magazine that he **shot his load**.

這男孩看色情雜誌看得很興奮，看到射出來了。

load something off on someone

3 片 動 把責任推到別人身上

The drug dealer knew that a narcotics agent was on to him, so he **loaded his drug deal off on someone** else. He wasn't going to go to jail for selling drugs.

毒販知道一名緝毒警察要逮捕他，於是他把罪行都栽贓到別人身上，他不想販毒被關。

get a load of

4 〔慣〕提醒對方注意某人或某物

Get a load of that guy. He just came out of the bathroom and left his fly open.

快看那個男的！他剛走出洗手間，石門水庫沒關。

get a load on

5 〔慣〕喝醉的

Jerry's **got a load on** and won't stop talking.

傑瑞喝醉了，講個不停。

　　load 最常見的用法是指「精液」，這是男生講到射精或高潮時，女生很少用這個詞，因為這説法很粗俗，而且也不是女生會做的事，它有點像是 locker-room phrase（更衣室裡説的話），男生在更衣室裡討論打手槍或做愛這類事時，他們會以 **shoot one's load** 來表達「高潮」。

109

loose [lus]

1 形 放鬆的

I need to relax and get **loose**. I've been really uptight lately over my studies.

我得好好放鬆一下，我最近為了課業一直很緊繃。

2 形 不負責任的

There's been a lot of **loose** talk lately among Western leaders about going to war in the Middle East.

最近有很多傳言說西方領袖打算要在中東開戰。

3 形 淫亂的

I wouldn't get too serious with that girl if I were you. I hear she's **loose**.

如果我是你的話，我不會對那個女孩太認真，聽說她是浪女。

　　loose 本意為「寬鬆的」，當俚語時，get loose 表示「放鬆心情」。

　　另外兩個俚語用法現今較不常用，loose talk 表示「閒談」，loose 也指「性生活很亂的女人」。

lose it

1 慣 失控、失去理智

Amber was driving the other night when she suddenly **lost it**. She couldn't think straight and had to swerve her car to avoid hitting a tree.

安柏前幾天晚上開車,突然腦袋糊塗了,結果差點撞上一棵樹。

2 慣 忍不住發飆

Heather often **loses it** with her little brother. He comes into her room without knocking, which makes her really mad.

海瑟常對她弟弟發飆,他不敲門就進她房間,讓她很氣。

lose one's cool

3 慣 發飆

The other day Frank **lost his cool** on another student. He was trying to figure out the math problem and the other student kept making fun of him.

前幾天法蘭克忍不住對一個學生發飆,因為他在解數學題目的時候,那個同學一直捉弄他。

lose one's marbles

4 慣 發瘋

When I was a little girl there was a woman known as Crazy Shirley who lived in our neighborhood. She **lost her marbles** when her husband died. She'd go to a restaurant and order a meal for two and then she'd talk to her deceased husband.

我小時候，我們附近住了一個女的，叫瘋狂雪莉。她先生去世後就瘋了。她會上餐廳點兩份餐，接著跟她已經去世的先生説話。

　　以上幾種説法在北美和英國都相當普遍，用 **lose it** 表示「失去控制」或是「發飆」的用法源自英國，雖然每個年齡層的人都會 lose it，但是這個詞多半是成人在用。

　　另外一個也可以表示「發飆」的有趣説法是 **lose one's cool**，如果一個人平時很鎮定，當他發飆，就可以用這個俚語提醒他！

　　如果你 **lose your marbles**，那問題就比 lose your cool 更嚴重，這時候你再也無法正常過生活了。這是不太禮貌的説法，表示你沒有能力自己處理事情。

　　在某些狀況下，可以當成笑話來説，例如你想去度假一週，跑去問老闆，他可能會對你説：「Have you lost your marbles?（你瘋了嗎？）」。

lush [lʌʃ]

1 名 酒鬼

Ben says he doesn't drink a lot, but everyone knows that he's a **lush**.

班說他不常喝酒，但大家都知道他是酒鬼。

2 形 超棒的食物、衣服、帥哥、美女

Check out that girl. She is **lush**.

看那個女的，她超正的。

Vodka and lime is **lush**; I'll have a treble, please!

萊姆伏特加超好喝，給我一杯三份量。

　　lush 是每個說英語的酒吧或舞廳裡都會用到的字，不管星期幾，你一定會在酒吧裡看到喝得爛醉的人。它最常用來指習慣喝酒且喝很兇的人。

　　在英國，lush 是「迷人的人或物」，我猜對一個 lush（酒鬼）來說，任何酒都是 lush（令人著迷）的！lush 源於 luscious，意為「甜美味香」或「性感迷人」，俚語用法和原意有直接的關聯。

make [mek]

1 名 核對身分

I will need to check the **make** and model of the car before I can tell you how much you'll need to pay for insurance.

我得先查一下車子的型號，才能告訴你要繳多少保費。

make out

2 片動 做愛；親熱

After the relationship was over, she realized that they had spent more time **making out** than doing anything else.

她跟男友分手以後，才發現他們上床親熱的時間比做其他事情的時間都要多。

make off with

3 片動 偷竊

The teenager **made off with** a bag of candy and a bottle of soda before the cashier knew it.

這名少年趁店員發現之前，偷走了一袋糖果和一瓶汽水。

最常見的兩個片語 **make out** 和 **make off with** 都源於英國。make out 可表示「做愛」，也可能只是親吻、愛撫，沒有走完全程。

marble ['marbl]

1

名 理智

Is it true that Mozart lost his **marbles** while composing his last symphony?

聽說莫札特在寫最後一首交響曲的時候瘋了，是真的嗎？

2

名 睪丸

The little boys were in karate class, and one of the boys accidentally kicked the other one in the **marbles**. He fell over in pain!

這群小男生正在一起學空手道，結果其中一個小男生踢到了另一個小男生的蛋蛋，讓他痛得趴在地上！

　　marble 原意是「彈珠」，當俚語表「理智」或「睪丸」，跟原意沒有關係。其中最常見的用法是「理智」，而且這多是祖父母輩的人在使用

　　用 marbles 表示「睪丸」則多是小學生、中學生在説，這個年齡的小孩還不曉得有更粗俗的字眼可以表達男性生殖器。

mega [ˋmɛgə]

1 形 **非常大的**

Mark signed a **mega** deal with a publishing company to publish his books.

馬克跟出版社簽了一個超大的約,要出版他的書。

2 形 **極好的、讚透的**

I went to the amusement park with my boyfriend and then out for dinner. We had a **mega** time!

我和男友去遊樂園玩,一起吃晚餐,真是超開心的一天!

mega 最常見的用法是指任何超大的事物。如果你用 mega 描述很讚的事物,此時 mega 多當成形容詞使用,如:

That ride was mega fun. Let's do it again!

剛才那個浪真過癮,再來一次!

150

mellow ['mɛlo]

1 形 放鬆的

After a long day at work I like to come home, turn on my music, and just get mellow.

工作一整天之後，我喜歡回家打開音樂，好好放鬆一下。

2 形 圓熟的；老練的

Sandra used to be tough and aggressive, but she's become mellow now that she's older.

珊卓以前很強硬、好鬥，現在年紀大了，變得比較圓滑了。

3 形 不緊繃、不壓抑

After yoga I always feel very mellow. I float all the way home and sleep peacefully.

每次做完瑜珈，我總覺得好放鬆，好像一路飄回家，睡得很安穩。

mellow out

4 片 動 變得安詳

You really need to get away and mellow out. Go to some island and just enjoy the water, sand, and surf.

你真的該離開這裡去散散心，去某個小島，享受海水、沙灘和衝浪。

mellow 和 mellow out 都是六〇年代就出現的詞，在那時候，be mellow 或 be chill 都是嬉皮會做的事或會說的話。今天想要 be mellow 或是要別人 mellow out 的，不只嬉皮了。

mob [mɑb]

1 名 幫派

Al Capone is known as one of the most dangerous **mob** bosses of all time. While he was in charge, he killed many and also had many killed.

艾爾‧卡彭是有史以來最危險的幫派老大之一，他當頭時幹掉了好多人。

mob scene

2 片 非常擁擠的狀況

Each year, the area outside where the Academy Awards ceremony is held turns into a **mob scene**. People want to see their favorite movie stars walk down the red carpet.

每年奧斯卡頒獎典禮會場外圍人山人海，大家都想看他們最愛的影星走星光大道。

　　如果你在美國講 mob，大家都會想到有組織的犯罪行為和暴力屠殺，雖然世界各地都有幫派組織，但是最出名的都在美國，他們通常都來自義大利或愛爾蘭。現在美國境內的幫派規模已不像過去龐大，但是一些有組織的犯罪集團依然存在。

　　因為幫派分子在人多的地方槍殺某人後，大家都會開始奔跑逃命，所以 mob scene 被用來形容場面一片混亂。

monkey around

1 片動 胡鬧、調皮、搗蛋

My little preschoolers always love to monkey around when we go on field trips. Since they are only three and four years old it is actually very cute.

我們出去郊遊時，我那兩個還沒上小學的孩子總愛調皮搗蛋，他們才三歲、四歲，其實蠻可愛的。

2 片動 胡來、亂動

I don't know the first thing about computers, so I just monkey around with mine in my spare time.

我對電腦一竅不通，所以我只好有空的時候胡亂摸索。

monkey business

3 名 不道德或不合法的行為

The owner of the company caught one of his employees doing some monkey business. Instead of reporting him to the police, he sacked him on the spot.

公司老闆抓到一個員工在搞鬼，他沒報警，但是當場把他開除了。

M

I will let you have a friend sleep over, but there had better not be any monkey business. When it is time to go to bed, you have to go to sleep.

我會讓你的朋友來這裡過夜，但是你們最好不要亂搞，該睡覺，你們就得乖乖睡覺。

　　大家都知道猴子喜歡跑來跑去、玩耍嬉鬧，然後大家都笑牠。monkey around 和 monkey business 的俚語意義在本質上和 monkey 的原意相當類似。如果有人在 monkey around（做愚蠢好笑的事），也不是什麼危險的事，但其他人可能會覺得有點煩，monkey around 會讓氣氛更輕鬆。

　　如果有人在做 monkey business（不恰當或不合法的行為），那我們就不能姑息，通常不是好事，往往會影響到他人。

moody ['mudɪ]

1 形 生氣的

I told Oscar he couldn't play today because he hit another student. He became **moody** and just sat in the corner pouting.

我跟奧斯卡説因為他打同學所以今天不能出去玩。他好生氣,嘟著嘴坐在角落。

2 形 喜怒無常的

I don't know how to handle Albert since he's become so **moody** lately. One minute he's fine and the next he is upset and ready to explode.

我不知道要怎麼跟艾柏特相處,最近他似乎特別情緒化。前一分鐘還好好的,下一分鐘他就氣炸了,隨時都要爆發。

3 形 憂鬱的

Some people say that certain bands sound dark and **moody**. They say that their music is sad and depressing.

有人説某些樂團聽起來很陰鬱,他們的音樂既悲傷又鬱悶。

　　如果有人説你很 **moody**,那你就該試著放輕鬆,別老擔心這擔心那的。moody 的人通常都不知道自己的情緒就跟雲霄飛車一樣,忽上忽下,對女性來説,每個月總有某些時候會讓她們特別陰晴不定。

muck [mʌk]

1

名 骯髒、灰塵

Phil forgot to take his shoes off when he came in and got **muck** all over my floor.

菲爾進門時忘了脫鞋，弄得我家地板都是髒東西。

2

名 品質低劣的東西

Why do you read this **muck**?

你為什麼要讀這種垃圾？

3

名 令人不愉快、冒犯的或沒價值的東西

Gayle loves watching reality shows. Personally, I don't know how she can watch that **muck**.

蓋兒很愛看真人實境秀，我不懂她怎麼能忍受那種無腦的東西。

 muck 通常只會在英國聽到，以上三種用法也都源於英國。其中最常用的說法是用來表示「骯髒、灰塵」。

muck about

1

 閒晃

On Tuesday nights I always **muck about** with my boyfriend's roommates.

我星期二晚上總會跟我男朋友的室友們到處閒晃。

muck in

2

 和別人分擔職責或工作

The children always **muck in** when it is time to clean up.

一到要打掃的時候,孩子們都會分工合作。

mucker

3

名 朋友

Jane and Nora are such good **muckers**. They gave me their shoulders to cry on when I broke up with my boyfriend.

珍和諾拉真是我的姊妹淘,我跟男友分手的時候,是她們在我身邊安慰我、支持我。

　　這些俚語起源於英國,其中最常見的是 muck about,從和朋友出去玩、逛街、看電影、到登山,都是 muck about。下次出去玩得很開心、想續攤時,就可以說你在 muck about,這樣度過下午很過癮,特別是和 mucker 一起 muck about! mucker 是英國及澳洲俚語。

muck up

1

片 動 毀壞、糟蹋

The outdoor wedding was **mucked up** when it began to rain heavily. All the flowers and chairs got drenched in the thunderstorm.

因為下大雨，戶外婚禮泡湯了，暴風雨讓所有的鮮花、椅子都濕透了。

2

片 動 笨手笨腳搞砸了工作

We ended up **mucking up** Cameron's surprise birthday party. We left an invitation message on his answering machine instead of his sister's.

我們最後把卡麥隆的生日派對驚喜搞砸了，我們本來要留言到他姊姊的答錄機，結果留到他的去了。

mucky

3

形 粗野的、無禮的

The waitress at the restaurant was really **mucky**. She practically threw the food at us.

餐廳裡那個女服務生超沒禮貌的，她根本就是把食物丟給我們。

這幾個字源於英國，在北美和其他地區都還不普遍，澳洲和紐西蘭也有類似的俚語，所以你在這些地區或是這些國家的英語人士口中，會聽到 muck 的各種不同用法。

其中最常用的是 **muck up**，可將情況想像為每回一轉身，自己和其他人都會被泥巴濺到，用來代表搞砸事情，這個字好玩的是它聽起來跟 fuck up 有點像，所以有些人聽到這個字會有些反感，不過你在公共場合還是可以用 muck up，不用擔心別人聽到。

122

069

nail [nel]

1
動 抓住某人

The police **nailed** the 7-Eleven robbers.
警察抓到了搶小七的搶匪。

2
動 打人或物

The scooter driver wasn't paying attention and **nailed** Jack.
機車騎士沒看路，結果撞到傑克。

3
動 上床

He didn't really care about her; he just wanted to **nail** her.
他根本不在乎她，只是想跟她上床。

4
動 完美達成某件事

Todd **nailed** the job interview.
托德面試大成功。

名 施打毒品的針頭

The junkie put the **nail** in his arm.
毒蟲把針頭扎進手臂裡。

　　看到名詞 **nail**，你會想到「釘子」，讓你可以把東西固定在某個地方，上述的俚語和原意有雷同之處。用 nail 表示「抓住」某人，就像是你把某人或某物固定住。

　　動詞 nail 則表示把釘子「釘」在木頭上的動作，這和 nail 的俚語用法「打」相當類似。

　　跟別人上床做愛的時候，也會有碰撞的動作，所以和 nail 的動詞原意也有關聯。但是 nail someone 或 be nailed 通常都帶有負面意味，用來描述性經驗也不是很好聽的講法。

　　nail 的動詞用法還可以指「完美做到某件事」。

nut [nʌt]

1 名 頭

Ray wasn't paying attention and hit his **nut** on the floor when he tripped and fell.

雷走路心不在焉，結果一跤摔倒在地上，撞到了頭。

2 名 怪人

Sue is such a **nut**. She often strikes up conversations with total strangers in the street.

蘇真是怪咖，常常跟街上的陌生人搭訕！

nuts

3 名 睪丸

When the man tried to attack Ivy, she kicked him in the **nuts** and ran away.

那個男的想欺負艾薇，艾薇踢中他的要害，趁機逃走。

4 形 瘋的

Are you **nuts**?

你瘋了嗎？

be nuts about

名 ⋯⋯迷；狂熱者

Some people **are nuts about** the *Transformers* movies. They'll camp out for weeks waiting in line for opening day.

有些人就是這麼迷《變形金剛》。他們會在外頭搭帳篷睡好幾個星期，排隊等首映。

6

慣 深愛

She **is nuts about** her new boyfriend.

她為新男友癡狂。

nut（堅果）不只可以吃，還可以用來表示很多不同的東西。nut 最常用來描述人，像是開玩笑地說別人是 nut（瘋子、怪人），不能指被診斷有精神病的人。

nut 還用來描述那些「影迷」、「球迷」、「做事方法與眾不同的人」以及「男生的蛋蛋」。

nutty

1

形 瘋瘋顛顛的

She's a good professor, perhaps a bit **nutty**, though.

她是個好教授,但或許有點瘋狂的。

nutter

2

名 瘋子

He is a **nutter**. When he gets angry, he always punches the wall.

他這人真是個瘋子,每次一生氣就捶牆壁。

nutcase

3

名 精神錯亂

The man was a total **nutcase**. Instead of sending him to prison, they sent him to an insane asylum.

那個男的發瘋了,他沒被關起來,而是被送進精神病院。

　　小時候為了看某個電視節目而想要晚點睡覺的時候,父母總會問我們是不是 **nutty**(瘋了)? 他們也知道不需要把我們送進醫院檢查,只要讓我們繼續看下一個節目就好了。

　　英國人用 **nutter** 的時候,並不一定指那些住在精神病院裡的人。你可以用 nutter 指稱這些人,但是它也可以用來戲謔地說對方是個傻瓜或瘋子,nutty 也是一樣。

off

1 🔹 幹掉；殺死

He was such a nutcase that he went and **offed** his entire family while they were sleeping. 他是個瘋子，把在睡覺的家人全都殺了。

off one's head

2 🔹 精神錯亂、瘋狂

She's completely **off her head** to talk to her boss in that disrespectful tone.

她用這麼不禮貌的口氣跟老闆說話，真是瘋了！

off one's block

3 🔹 愚蠢

Are you **off your block**? I'm not jumping into that freezing cold water! 你瘋啦？我才不要跳進凍死人的水裡咧！

off one's face

4 🔹 酒後或吸毒後的興奮狀態

I never saw so many people **off their faces** like I did the other night at the concert.

我從來沒看過像前幾天晚上的演唱會那樣，有那麼多人吸毒嗨翻。

off one's box

慣 喝醉酒

Jeremy was so **off his box** after a night of drinking that he fell and knocked his nut. He had a big lump on his head the next morning and a bad headache.

傑瑞米喝太醉了，結果跌倒撞到頭。隔天早上他頭上腫了一個包，頭痛得很厲害。

　　如果你 off（幹掉）了某人，被解決掉的人通常是你認識的人，幫派分子常用這個字。用 off 描述「死」是很殘酷無情的，不是美好的死法，也沒有平靜安詳的感覺，大多是謀殺。

　　off one's head 和 **off one's block** 兩者可以互換使用，off one's head 開玩笑地説人「瘋狂」、「古怪」，而非形容真正的精神病患。

　　如果對方向你提出請求時，**off one's block** 是個有趣的回答。小孩想做什麼，父母不答應時，大人往往就會用 off one's block 回答小孩。這都是有點開玩笑的説法。

　　off one's box 和 **off one's face** 很相似，兩者都是指人受酒或毒品影響；off one's face 來自澳洲，它可指「喝醉酒」，但還是多用來指「吸毒後的迷惘狀態」。

off the hook

1 慣 **擺脫麻煩**

John used to get into trouble all the time with his parents, and his older brother would be the one to get him **off the hook**.

約翰以前老是惹爸媽生氣，他大哥總會幫他脫身。

2 慣 **免於責任**

My boss had asked me to work overtime on Tuesday, but my colleague volunteered to do it, so luckily, I was **off the hook**.

我老闆叫我週二加班，但我同事自告奮勇，很幸運地，我逃過一劫了。

3 慣 **好到難以形容**

The new album is so **off the hook**. It's like nothing I've ever heard before!

這張新專輯真是棒透了，我以前從沒聽過這麼讚的音樂！

off the wall

4 形 **新穎的、不尋常的**

The movie is an **off-the-wall** comedy that both kids and adults will enjoy.　這電影是個不尋常的喜劇，大人小孩都愛看。

　　off the hook 的俚語用法全都源於北美洲，似乎興起過後又退流行。如果你的父母或老師使用 off the hook，多半是因為你做錯了什麼事，但是他們這次特別通融，所以你不必受罰。現在你會聽到年輕人用 off the hook 描述瘋狂的音樂、電影或經驗，這個用法是饒舌歌手重新引進的，他們把很棒的事形容為 off the hook。**off the wall** 含有貶義，成年人使用 off the wall 的頻率會比 off the hook 高。

payoff ['pe,ɔf]

1 **名** 結果、結局

She knew if she studied hard and did well on the entrance exams the **payoff** would be great.

她知道如果用功唸書，入學考試考得好，最後就會有好結果。

2 **名** 犯罪所得

The bank robbers walked away with a **payoff** of over one and a half million dollars.　銀行搶匪帶著一百五十多萬美金離開了。

3 **名** 提供服務所得到的報酬

After the couple found the home of their dreams, they gave the real estate agent the **payoff**. They only had to pay 20% up front for her services.　這對夫婦找到他們夢寐以求的房子後，付給房仲一筆報酬，但其實他們只須預付 20% 的仲介費。

4 **名** 應得的獎賞或懲罰

It was about time he saw a **payoff** for all the horrible things he has done. I don't feel bad at all for what happened to him.

現在應該要讓他知道他做這些可怕的事會得到什麼報應了，我一點都不可憐他。

payoff 最常出現的用法為「應得的報酬」；payoff 常指金錢上的報酬、言語上的回報。但不是所有 payoff 都是好的，「應得的懲罰」就是不好的，像做壞事的代價可能就是被 offed（幹掉）。

peck [pɛk]

1 動 小口小口地咬

Christina never eats heartily. She'll **peck** at her food as if she wasn't hungry.

克里絲汀娜從不會盡情大吃,只會小口小口咬,好像一點也不餓。

2 名 匆匆一吻

She hated that their last kiss ever was only a **peck** on the lips. She longed for one of their passionate kisses.

她想到他們最後一個吻只是輕吻就覺得討厭,她渴望以前那種熱吻。

　　用 **peck** 表示「小口的咬」衍生自鳥啄食的動作,牠們嘴巴很小所以啄的量很少,且動作快速,這和 peck 常用的俚語用法「匆匆一吻」和「小口吃東西」有雷同之處。
　　臉頰上的 peck 通常是家人給的,但也可能發生在一段戀情剛開始或快結束時的尷尬處境。

piece [pis]

1

名 藝術創作

Did you see the **piece** on the side of the bridge? I love all the colors!

你有沒有看到橋邊的塗鴉？我愛它的用色。

2

名 槍

When the police came, the man dropped his **piece**.

條子一來，那男的趕緊丟槍。

3

名 性伴侶、上床對象

Some men feel that the only thing women are good for is a **piece**. They use them and never get to know who they really are.

有些男人覺得女人唯一的用途就是上床，只利用女人，從來都不知道這些女人到底是什麼樣的人。

　　這個字永遠不會退流行，時時都有人在想辦法要得到 a piece of something（一塊、一份……），不過若你把 **piece** 當俚語時，就只能指三樣東西——「街頭塗鴉」、「槍」和「性伴侶」。

　　用 piece 指「槍」多是持槍者、警察和饒舌歌手在用。年輕一代比較常用 piece 的俚語用法。

　　piece 指「性伴侶」，通常是說那些只被視為上床對象的女人，這個用法很粗俗，物化女性，不能亂用。

pig [pɪg]

1 名 條子；警察

I got pulled over by a **pig** last night. I didn't have my lights on and when he asked for my driver's license I didn't have it on me.

昨晚我沒開大燈，被條子攔了下來，他要我出示駕照，我才發現我根本沒帶。

2 名 沙豬男

Henry is such a **pig**. He is always trying to pick up girls at the bar, and he treats them disrespectfully.

亨利真是個沙豬男，他每次都在酒吧釣美眉，對她們很不尊重。

3 名 貪心的人

Roger behaved like a **pig**. He took all the food at the table and didn't offer anyone else anything.

羅傑很貪心，把桌上所有食物都拿走，完全不分別人一點。

4 名 又胖又醜的人

That woman on the bus looked like a **pig**. I felt sorry for her because it seemed she hadn't taken care of herself in months.

我真為公車上那恐龍妹難過，因為她看起來好像好幾個月沒好好照顧自己了。

　　可愛的 **pig**（豬）怎麼會得到這麼糟的名聲？這個字有好幾種用法，且都不是用來稱讚人的。在美國用 pig 稱呼警察，不過這可是很冒犯警察的暱稱，不可當面說。

　　第二常見的用法則是專給女性使用的，它用來描述對女性無禮又粗魯的男人，或是只把女性視為上床對象的男人。英國人會用 pig 指「醜女人」或「貪心的人」。

piss [pɪs]

1

名 小便、尿

He got up from the table and announced to everyone that he had to take a **piss**. It was so inappropriate.

他從桌邊站起來，跟大家說他要去尿尿，真是失禮。

2

名 品質很差的酒

This beer is **piss**! Get me another one from the fridge.

這啤酒喝起來就像尿一樣！從冰箱給我拿別的來！

3

名 胡說、廢話

That is a load of **piss**! I never said that!

滿口胡說！我才沒說過那些話！

piss away

4

片動 浪費、揮霍

He is such a great guy; it's a shame he is **pissing** his life **away**.

他這個人不錯，可惜老是在浪費生命。

piss down

5 片動 下大雨

With the typhoon coming, it was **pissing down** all day yesterday.

颱風來了，所以昨天整天都在下大雨。

piss 有時會冒犯人，有些人把它看成髒話，就看你怎麼說了，它最常用來表示「小便」。人人都得上小號，尿急的人會用這個字來公告緊急狀況。

piss away 指「浪費」、「揮霍」，用來形容具體或抽象的事物都可以。

piss in the wind

1 慣 徒勞無功

Trying to get into the top medical school in the country is like **pissing in the wind**. My grades are definitely not good enough.

想進國家一流的醫學院簡直是難如登天，我的成績絕對上不了。

piss on it

2 慣 忘掉某事、不再管它

I already told him that he's making a big mistake by quitting school, but he won't listen to me so **piss on it**!

我已經跟他說過，輟學是個大錯，但他不肯聽勸，管他的！

piss oneself

3 慣 狂笑

The comedian was so funny I nearly **pissed myself**.

這個喜劇演員差點讓我笑到尿褲子。

如果你在逆風時小便，你就會懂 **piss in the wind** 為什麼表示「不管怎麼做，都不會成功」，因為你一定會被自己的尿灑到。

piss on it 表示你不想管了，也不想在乎某事了。

如果你曾經笑到尿褲子，你就會知道 **piss oneself** 是什麼意思了，用於英國。

piss off

1 片動 惹惱別人

With all of her childish antics, she ended up **pissing** everyone **off**.

她所有幼稚滑稽的舉動最終把大家惹火了。

2 片動 走開

I just want you to **piss off** and leave me alone. I don't want to talk to anyone right now.

我只想要你走開，讓我靜一靜，我現在不想跟任何人說話。

pissed

3 形 喝醉的

The whole rugby team got **pissed** after their victorious game on Saturday.

星期六贏球之後，所有英式橄欖球隊隊員都喝醉了。

pissed off

4 形 生氣的

I'm so **pissed (off)** that he broke my bicycle. I refuse to talk to him now.

我很氣他弄壞了我的腳踏車，我現在不想跟他說話。

5 慣 失望的

Ted's **pissed off** with his life. He hates his job and just broke up with his girlfriend.

泰德對自己的人生感到很失望,他厭惡自己的工作,最近又跟女友分手。

「生氣」用 **pissed (off)** 有點粗俗,但能夠傳達你有多憤怒,「惹火別人」則是用 piss someone off。

英國、澳洲、紐西蘭用 **pissed** 表「喝醉的」,但北美只用來表「生氣或失望」。

pissy ['pɪsi]

1 形 不耐煩或生氣

Tom said he didn't see why Paul was being so **pissy**.
湯姆說他不曉得為何保羅這麼生氣。

2 形 不重要的、瑣碎的、地位低下的

I don't know why I even care about this breakup. In the grand scheme of things, it was a **pissy** three months of my life.
我真不知道我為什麼這麼在乎這次分手，這只不過是我人生中短短的三個月。

pissy drunk

3 形 喝得大醉

Dora got **pissy drunk** last night.
朵拉昨晚喝掛了。

pissy 一般字典查不到，它的意思是「心情不好」，通常是不耐煩或生氣。

若要形容「喝得很醉」或「喝掛」，常用 **pissy drunk**，屬口語，少用於書面。

plant [plænt]

1 動 揍一拳

The boxer **planted** a nice one right in the middle of his opponent's face. It knocked him out and he won the match.

拳擊手一拳打中對手的臉,把對方擊倒,贏得比賽。

2 動 埋葬

I don't like the idea of retirement. In fact, I'm going to keep on working until they **plant** me.

我不喜歡退休,事實上,我打算工作到他們把我埋進土裡為止。

　　這裡的 **plant** 可不是地上長出來的「植物」或「種植」。當俚語時,plant 是指在對方的臉上、肚子上或其他地方「揍一拳」,如果你 plant one on someone,那你就是真的狠狠地揍了對方。

　　另一個俚語用法是指「埋葬」,這和原意很接近,像植物種在土裡一樣,埋葬也算是另類地把人種在地底下。

plastered [ˈplæstɚd]

1 勔 大力擊倒

Rick not only lost the boxing match, but he got totally **plastered** by his opponent.

瑞克不只輸掉拳擊賽，還被對手徹底擊倒。

2 形 喝醉的

Al always gets **plastered** when he goes out with the guys on weekends.

艾爾週末和他那群朋友出去，每次都會喝到掛。

3 形 猛烈射擊、猛烈砲轟

During times of war, cities and towns get **plastered**, innocent people die, and homes and businesses get destroyed.

戰爭期間，城市和鄉鎮遭到猛烈轟炸，無辜百姓犧牲了性命，家園和產業也都被摧毀。

　　plaster原意「灰泥」，用來塗在牆上堅固牆面。最常用的俚語用法源於美國。基本上，如果你 **plastered**（喝醉酒、被擊倒）了，唯一可以做的事就是靠在牆上！

　　plastered用來表示「猛烈射擊」或「猛烈轟炸」，在一般日常生活中你不會聽到這個用法，但是軍隊裡會用這個字，特別是戰爭期間。

plug [plʌg]

1
名 衛生棉條

Hey, Jill, do you have an extra **plug**? It's that time of the month again.

嘿！吉兒，你有沒有多的棉條？我那個來了。

2
動 打一拳

An innocent bystander got **plugged** right in the head during some brawl after a rugby game.

英式橄欖球賽結束後，一名無辜的旁觀者被打架的人一拳打到頭。

3
動 用槍射擊

When the boys were younger, they would **plug** soda cans and beer bottles out behind the barn.

這些男生小時候會在穀倉後面用槍射擊汽水罐和啤酒瓶。

4
動 大打廣告

The singer went on several talk shows to **plug** his new album.

歌手上了幾個脫口秀，大力推薦他的新專輯。

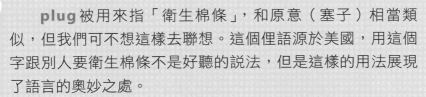

　　plug 被用來指「衛生棉條」，和原意（塞子）相當類似，但我們可不想這樣去聯想。這個俚語源於美國，用這個字跟別人要衛生棉條不是好聽的說法，但是這樣的用法展現了語言的奧妙之處。

　　plug 當動詞用時，可以指「打一拳」或「用槍射擊」，以及「在廣播或電視中大力推銷某種商品」。

pot [pɑt]

1 名 廁所

Before we leave, let me run to the **pot**. It's going to be a long car ride.

我們出門前,先讓我去趟廁所吧!我們要坐很久的車。

2 名 大麻

A lot of people are trying to legalize **pot**.

很多人想讓大麻合法化。

pothead

3 名 大麻癮君子

My college roommate was a **pothead**. It's a miracle that he actually graduated.

我大學室友是大麻癮君子,他能畢業真是奇蹟。

pot 是「大麻」的暱稱,如果你抽大麻,那你就是個 **pothead**。如果你自己有抽,就不會覺得這是個罵人的字,因為它單純地就是指「抽大麻的人」。你也可能會聽到那些不抽大麻的人用 pothead 批評抽大麻的人!不過不是每個人都是 pothead,這個字是用來指那些不只偶爾抽抽,而是抽大麻抽上癮的人。

psych up

1 片動 讓自己做好準備

The Olympic runner **psyched** himself **up** before the race.

奧運賽跑選手在比賽前做足準備。

2 片動 使某人對某事物作好心理準備

With all the rumors she heard about her boyfriend, Abigail **psyched** herself **up** to believe the worst.

艾比蓋兒聽到男友的所有緋聞以後，她做了最壞的打算。

psych out

3 片動 使氣餒

In order to beat his opponent, he had to **psych** him **out**. He did this by talking shit to him while on the field.

為了擊敗對手，他要挫對方銳氣，所以他在場上向他罵髒話。

　　psych up 和 **psych out** 兩個俚語有點像是文字遊戲。psych 是 psychological（心理學的）的簡稱，用來描述任何和心理學或與個人情緒及行為特徵有關的現象。

　　如果你想改變情緒或行為，就要改變思考和感覺的方式，可透過跟自己對話或是激勵自己超越極限而達到。這也是為什麼我們說 psych yourself/oneself up，你得進入自己或別人的腦中，使自己或別人產生不同於平時的思考和感覺。這兩個說法在運動員、學生和音樂家之間都很常用。

punk [pʌŋk]

1 名 替小孩或青少年取的暱稱

I'm not going to let that little **punk** tell me what to do. He needs to show some respect.

我才不讓那個小鬼告訴我怎麼做,他要尊重我才對。

2 名 小混混、小流氓

Carl acts like he's a tough, powerful criminal, but he's just a **punk**.

卡爾表現得好像很兇惡的罪犯,但他只不過是個小混混。

punk 可以用來半開玩笑地形容「小孩」,通常只會讓對方了解到說話者對他們持有的態度。punk 用來指「小混混」,帶有貶義。

put down

1 片動 侮辱某人

My husband is always **putting** me **down** in front of our friends. That's not very respectful.

我先生老是在朋友面前羞辱我，真的很不尊重我。

put one's nose out of joint

2 慣 傷害某人的自尊

Coming in second place in the competition **put Jason's nose out of joint**, so he didn't want to go to the reception dinner afterward.

比賽只拿到第二名讓傑森沒面子，所以他不想去接下來的晚宴。

put on

3 片動 開玩笑、惡作劇

Tiffany couldn't believe she won the all-expense-paid trip to Australia when the radio announcer told her. She thought he was just **putting** her **on**.

蒂芬妮聽到電台主持人說她贏了全程免費的澳洲旅遊，簡直不敢相信，以為是在開玩笑。

4 片動 假裝

She was so upset but she couldn't let anyone know. She wiped away her tears, **put on** a smile, and went back out to the party.

她心裡很難過，但是她不能讓別人知道；她擦去淚水，強裝微笑，回到派對上。

put away

5 片動 幹掉某人

The mob boss threatened to **put** me **away** if I didn't give him back the money I owed him.

幫派老大恐嚇我，如果我不還錢就把我幹掉。

6 片動 坐牢

The man was **put away** for life for murder.

那男的因謀殺被判無期徒刑。

這幾個很常用的俚語都源於美國，用來表達負面意義。它們表面很相似，但是意義完全不同。

如果有人侮辱你，他們就是在 **put you down**；如果有人開你玩笑，他就是在 **put you on**；有人傷了你的自尊或冒犯你，那你的 **nose** 就有可能被 **put out of the joint**。

這當中最少用的是 **put someone away**（殺死某人）。電影裡聽到這個俚語的機會比真實生活來得多。

如果了解 on、out、away 的意義，就不難理解這些俚語的意思了。

080

R and R

1 🟦 休息放鬆

Carrie went on a much-needed vacation. She went to a tiny island in Thailand for some **R and R**.

凱莉放了一個很需要放的假，跑去泰國一個小島休息放鬆去了。

I love summer

2 🟦 搖滾樂

I once saw a guy with a tattoo of a guitar with the words, "I love **R & R**," in the middle of it. I wonder why he didn't just spell out the words.

有一次我看到一個男的身上刺了一把吉他，中間還有「I love R & R」這幾個字，我不懂為什麼不把 Rock and Roll 直接拼出來。

　　R and R 俚語簡單又切中要點，人們大都會直接說出 rock and roll。一般 R and R 最常用來表示 rest and relaxation（休息和放鬆）。多數人不會說 rest and relaxation，而常就只說 R and R。

rack one's brain

1 慣 努力回想

I **racked my brain** trying to remember the actor's name; then it suddenly came to me the next day.

我一直在想那個演員的名字，隔天就突然想起來了。

rack out

2 片動 躺下、睡覺

After a long day of hiking and swimming, Darren was ready to **rack out** as soon as he got home.

一天下來爬山又游泳，達倫一到家就準備睡覺了。

rack off

3 片動 被激怒、惹惱

Jane was so **racked off** by the salesperson's behavior that she decided to go somewhere else to make her purchase.

珍被店員弄得很不爽，所以她決定去別家店買東西。

rack up

4 片動 獲利或累積得分

The company **racked up** nearly two million dollars in profit last year.

公司去年累積獲利將近 200 萬元。

The team **racked up** five points in the second half of the game.

這隊下半場比賽就累積了五分。

rack one's brain 表示你絞盡腦汁，卻怎麼也想不起來某件事，通常只會搖自己的腦袋，不會用在別人身上。

racked off（被惹惱）源於英國，它的意義和 pissed off 很相似，但是比 pissed off 更適合在公共場合中使用，也比較不會冒犯到別人。

rad [ræd]

1 ⑱ 很好的

"How was your vacation?" "It was **rad**; I went to a bunch of islands and enjoyed scuba diving and snorkeling!"

「你假期過得怎麼樣？」

「好極了。我跑去好幾個小島玩，還去深潛和浮潛！」

2 ⑱ 流行的、時髦的

The new line of clothing for this season is really **rad**. The designs and colors are similar to the ones from the early eighties.

這一季新裝都好時髦，設計和顏色都和八〇年代早期的風格很像。

3 ⑱ 有趣的

I took a really **rad** bike ride through the city the other day. I saw things I hadn't seen before.

我前幾天騎腳踏車在市區逛得挺開心的，看到好多以前沒看過的東西。

radical

4 ⑱ 優異的、出色的

I saw the most **radical** band the other night. I had never heard of them before but they are going to be big one day.

前幾天晚上我聽到了一個超讚的樂團，我以前沒有聽過，不過他們有一天一定會成名！

 rad 源於美國，來自於 radical，兩者間並沒什麼差別，但是人們多只說 rad。這個字就是用來形容很棒的事物。

rag [ræg]

1

名 報紙

Their Sunday morning ritual consisted of sleeping in, making breakfast, and reading the Sunday **rag** on the terrace.

他們星期天作息比平常晚起、做早餐，然後在露臺上看星期天的報紙。

2

名 衛生棉

Celia prefers to use a tampon over a **rag**.

西莉亞比較愛用衛生棉條，不愛衛生棉。

3

名 劇院舞台上的幕

Brandy always loved when the **rag** went up on opening night. It was the beginning of many more nights doing what she loved.

布蘭迪最喜愛的就是首演當晚布幕升起的那一刻，那代表她接下來好幾個晚上又可以繼續做她喜歡做的事。

rag on

4 片動 嘲笑

Andrea's older sister was constantly **ragging on** her about her weight and appearance.

安卓雅的姊姊老是嘲笑她的體重和外表。

5 片動 嚴厲批評

The host began **ragging on** the government.

主持人開始大肆批評政府。

　　rag 最古老的用法是「報紙」，通常新聞界的人才會說 daily rag（日報）。另一個意義「舞台上的布幕」，只有劇場或百老匯的人才會用，一般人則直接用 curtain，不用 rag。

rage [redʒ]

1 玩得很開心

You've been working too hard, man. Let's go out this weekend and **rage** till the sun comes up.

老兄，你工作太辛苦了，我們週末去徹夜狂歡吧！

2 爆怒

After he drank too much he would **rage** at anyone who looked at him. He always got kicked out of bars.

他一喝太多，就對每個看他的人大發脾氣，常因此被轟出酒吧。

年輕的一代常常使用這個字。有時候你甚至可以同時使用這些俚語用法，如：

You can **rage** with your friends, and see someone get drunk and then get in a fit of **rage** and start screaming or yelling and possibly even start a fight with someone there.

你可以跟一票朋友去狂歡，然後看別人喝醉酒、發酒瘋，開始大吼大叫，甚至和人打架。

raghead

1 名 阿拉伯人或回教徒

After September 11, 2001, a lot of racism was directed towards people from the Middle East. Some people would make racial slurs and use the word "**raghead**."

2001 年 911 事件之後，很多人開始歧視中東民族。有些人甚至侮辱中東人，還用 raghead 的字眼來稱呼他們。

ragtop

2 名 敞篷車

My friend Matt has a red **ragtop**. I love driving around with him in the summer.

我朋友麥特有一台紅色敞篷車，夏天我很愛跟他一起去兜風。

raggedy-ass

3 形 寒酸、破舊的

Justin wears such **raggedy-ass** clothes. He really needs to buy some new clothing.

賈斯汀穿得很邋遢，真的該買新衣服了。

glad rags

4 名 慶祝場合穿的衣服

Tonight is a big night for Jessie, so she went out and bought some **glad rags**.

今天晚上是潔西的大日子，所以她出門買了幾件禮服。

raghead 用來稱呼阿拉伯人或回教徒已經多年了，它帶有種族歧視的意味，隨著人們對於中東民族敵對意識的上升，現在你可能會越常聽到很多人說這個字，但以北美人士使用得最多。

在北美，如果有人説我 **raggedy-ass**，我會覺得非常不高興，因為這代表我極為貧困，穿得破破爛爛的。

rake through

1 片動 仔細搜尋

When Olivia lost her engagement ring, she **raked through** the entire house trying to find it.

奧莉薇在家裡把訂婚戒指弄丟了，翻遍家中要把戒指找出來。

rake one's fingers through one's hair

2 片動 用手指撥頭髮

Raking her fingers through her hair, Carla thought about all the work she had to do that afternoon.

卡拉一邊用手梳頭髮，一邊想她那天下午要做的工作。

rake it in

3 慣 賺很多錢

A lot of people decide to teach English in a foreign country because the cost of living is less there than in their native countries, and it's easy for them to **rake it in**.

很多人決定到外國教英語，因為那裡生活開銷比自己的國家低，這樣很容易賺大錢。

rake someone over the coals

4 慣 大罵

Liz's father **raked her over the coals** when she told him she wouldn't be going back to school because she lost her scholarship.

麗茲跟爸爸說因為獎學金沒了，所以不想繼續上學，被她爸爸大罵一頓。

　　英國人會用 **rake through** 表示「仔細搜尋」，不過別的地方還是可以聽到這種用法。

　　rake 最常見的兩個俚語用法都源於美國，**rake it in**（賺大錢）和 **rake someone over the coals**（大罵）。每個人都想 rake it in，如果你想一想 rake（耙）的動作，就會發現這個說法還挺有道理的，看到錢，誰不想拿耙子把錢都耙在一起呢？

　　如果你曾經被人 rake over the coals，就是被大罵、訓斥一頓，罵別人則是用 rake someone over the coals。

random [ˈrændəm]

1 形 古怪的、反常的

The most **random** thing happened the other day. Jane was walking down the street when this guy stopped her and asked if she would do a photo shoot for his clothing line.

前幾天發生了一件奇事，珍走在路上遇到一個男的攔住她，問她願不願意為他的服飾品牌拍照。

2 形 陌生的

Sally gets so irritated when **random** guys come up and start talking to her.

每次有陌生男子過來跟莎莉搭話，就會惹毛她。

3 形 奇妙的、無法預料的

I met my ex-boyfriend in the most **random** situation. We were at a club listening to a band and someone in the crowd pushed us into one another.

我跟前男友是在很偶然的情況下認識的，我們在一間酒吧裡聽一個樂團表演，結果人群中有人把我們兩個推在一起。

　　random 源於美國。random 很好玩，其行為往往會帶來有趣的結果，和一個陌生人相識或偶遇，就可以視為一件 random 的事。我發覺我這輩子裡最有趣的時光，就是最意想不到的事發生的時候。

rank [ræŋk]

1 形 噁心的

The smell of the moldy food that I got out of the refrigerator was so **rank** that I almost threw up.

我從冰箱拿出來的食物發霉超噁心的,我差點就吐了。

2 動 羞辱、批評

She is so tired of her boss **ranking** on her when she asks him questions about the project she is working on.

每次她問老闆她手上案子的問題,老闆老愛出言羞辱,她真是煩死了。

這兩個俚語用法都源於美國,其中最常見的用法是「噁心的」,用來形容味道或氣味。

rank 表示「奚落」、「侮辱」,是黑人常用的俚語。

rap [ræp]

1 名 饒舌音樂

One of the most popular forms of music these days is **rap**. It has moved from out of the ghettos where it began and is now listened to by many people.

現今最流行的一種音樂類型就是饒舌樂，它從貧民區起家，現在很多人都愛聽。

2 名 罪責

The criminal pinned the murder **rap** on his partner.

這名罪犯指控他同夥犯下謀殺罪。

3 名 判以徒刑

The killer got a **rap** of life without parole.

兇手被判無期徒刑，不得假釋。

　　rap 是饒舌音樂，從紐約和洛杉磯這些大城市的貧民區開始發展。饒舌歌手藉音樂表達現實生活的遭遇，敘述了性、殺戮、欺騙、偷竊和被警察歧視等種種不平，現在已成為一種主流音樂，而饒舌歌手也遍布美國各地，不再限於大城市。

rat on

1 片動 告發、背叛某人

Nick got in trouble with his parents for smoking cigarettes because his sister **ratted on** him.

姊姊出賣尼克，說他抽菸，害尼克跟爸媽起衝突。

rat out

2 片動 遺棄、丟下

Jeff said he'd help us organize the party, but he **ratted out** the last minute.

傑夫說他會幫我們辦派對，結果到了最後一刻他丟下我們。

rat pack

3 慣 不良少年組成的幫派

Back in the old days when he was a teenager, Mel belonged to the neighborhood **rat pack**. He was pretty tough and got into some trouble, but as he got older, he began to mellow out.

梅爾青少年時是個街頭小混混，兇神惡煞，惹了不少麻煩，越來越大以後，他開始變得比較溫和。

rat race

4 🔊 無休無止的競爭

After having worked as a stock broker on Wall Street for over ten years, Stan decided to quit his job, move to the country, and get out of the **rat race**.

在華爾街當了超過十年的股票經紀人，史丹決定辭職搬到鄉下，離開無止境的競爭。

rat on指「告發、背叛」，而**rat out**指「丟下、遺棄」。用rat來說別人，多半是在罵對方為人不好或是無法信賴。

rat pack指小混混、不良少年組成的幫派。

rat race常形容極度競爭的工作，人為了一點小小的獎勵，無止盡的追逐。

rave [rev]

1 動 熱烈的讚美和鼓掌

Everyone has been **raving** about this restaurant, but I went there for lunch last week and didn't find the food to be all that good.

大家極力誇讚這間餐廳,但我上週去吃午餐,並不覺得有這麼好吃。

2 動 狂歡

Allen **raved** the entire time he was on vacation. He met a lot of people, drank a lot, and had a blast.

艾倫整個假期都在狂歡,認識了好多人,喝酒作樂。

3 名 充斥毒品的大型派對

There's going to be a big **rave** on the beach this weekend. Everyone will be there!

這個週末海邊要辦一個大型派對,每個人都會去喔!

4 名 流行、風尚

Gangnam style became all the **rave** around 2012, putting K-pop on the international map.

江南 Style 在 2012 年風靡全球,
讓韓國流行音樂登上國際舞台。

raver [ˈrevɚ]

5 名 社交生活狂野不羈的人

The **raver** danced nonstop to the beat of techno music, waving her glow sticks and high on ecstasy.

那 high 咖跟著電音舞曲跳個不停,揮舞螢光棒,嗑藥頭丸。

rave 指「狂歡趴踢」,是那種大型,有電子音樂,很多人會吸毒嗑藥的派對,最普遍的毒品就是搖頭丸(ecstasy),而參加這種派對的人就叫 raver,就是愛跑趴的人。

rave 表示「流行」、「時尚」,源於英國,現在較少用。

154

raw [rɔ]

1 形 粗俗的；粗野的

I couldn't believe Eddie used such **raw** language in front of my mother. She was absolutely offended and told him to leave the house immediately.

我真不敢相信艾迪在我媽面前飆粗話，我媽覺得受到冒犯，叫他立刻走人。

raw meat

2 名 只被視為上床對象的人

Jenny can't tell the difference between guys who see her only as **raw meat** and those who are genuinely interested in a relationship with her.

珍妮無法分辨哪個男生只想跟她上床，哪個男生真的要跟她談戀愛！

raw deal

3 慣 不公平的交易

Jeff got a **raw deal** when he bought his plane tickets right before the ticket prices went down.

傑夫買完機票，票價就立刻就降了，被虧到了。

如果有人形容你是 **raw meat**，對方認為你只是被當成「上床對象」，帶有貶義。

如果有人進行了不公平的交易，就可以說他 **get a raw deal**。

right on

1 嘆 **熱情的同意或贊成**

"I got Sheila to go out on a date with me."

"**Right on**, bro! I knew you'd do it."

「席拉答應跟我去約會了。」

「水啦，老弟！我就知道你會這麼做。」

2 形 **最新的；切題的**

What the politician said was **right on**. We need to be spending less on war and more on the poor folks in this country.

這名政治人物所說的一針見血，我們國家應該把錢多花在窮人身上，少花錢打仗。

righteous [ˈraɪtʃəs]

3 形 **傑出的**

That was one kick-ass film! Jason Statham's got some **righteous** moves. Did you see him cream those guys?

這部電影超棒的，傑森・史塔森的動作好厲害，你有沒有看到他怎麼打敗那些人的？

Right on!（完全同意！）這在八〇年代曾是最酷最炫的字，但是現在已經被其他的字取代，現在還是會聽到，但多是八〇年代那一代的人在說。

righteous 當俚語時，用來表示「很傑出」，八〇年代後期、九〇年代初期，美國黑人常用這個字，現在比較少用了。

ringer ['rɪŋɚ]

1 🔲 **幾乎一模一樣的人或物**

The guy Sharon saw the other night was a dead **ringer** for her cousin Matthew. She went up to him thinking it was Matthew.

雪倫前幾天晚上看到一個男的，長得跟她表弟麥修一模一樣，她以為是她表弟，還跑去找他。

2 🔲 **外觀和車牌都被更改的贓車**

It only took the car thieves two days to have the **ringer** completed and back out on the street for sale.

偷車賊只花了兩天，就把贓車改頭換面，送回街上去賣。

3 🔲 **槍手**

During the Little League World Series, teams would actually have **ringers**. The reason they did this was because the good players were too old.

在世界少棒錦標賽期間，球隊都會找槍手代打，因為好球員都超齡了。

　　dead ringer 表示兩個人或物看起來長得一模一樣，這裡的 dead 意思是絲毫不差的，跟死沒關係。

　　ringer 表示「贓車」，多是警方或偷車賊的行話，一般人在日常生活中很少會這麼說。

　　ringer 表示「代人比賽的槍手」是運動圈的行話，槍手是祕密，所以你不會聽到有人公開說誰誰誰是 ringer。賽馬時，頂替另一匹馬上陣比賽的馬匹，也是 ringer。

rip-off [ˈrɪpˌɔf]

1 名 冒牌貨

Can't you see that's not a real Rolex watch? It's just a cheap **rip-off**.

你看不出那是假的勞力士錶嗎？那是便宜的山寨版。

2 名 價錢過高的商品

I went to the night market the other day to buy some cantaloupe. I couldn't believe what a **rip-off** it was. I would never spend that much on fruit!

我前幾天去夜市去買香瓜，那裡的香瓜根本就是在搶錢，我絕不會花大錢買水果！

3 名 詐騙、騙局

The secondhand smartphone I bought was a total **rip-off**. It stopped working the minute I took it home.

我買的二手智慧型手機根本是詐騙，我帶回家就壞掉了。

rip off

4 片動 偷取

Albert's bike was parked at the MRT station on Sunday night and it got **ripped off**. This is the second time it happened to him in three months.

艾柏特禮拜天晚上把腳踏車停在捷運站，結果被偷了，這已經是三個月內第二次被偷了。

5 片動 敲竹槓；剝削

The vendors at the street market are known to **rip off** unsuspecting tourists.

這條街市上的攤販以敲詐無防備之心的遊客聞名。

如果你說某物是 **rip-off**，要不是買貴了，就是買到冒牌貨。

如果你的東西被偷了，你可以說：

I was **ripped off** when I was at the airport.

在機場的時候，我東西被偷了。

ripe [raɪp]

1 形 臭的

The garbage needs to be taken out. It is gathering flies and smells pretty **ripe**.

垃圾該拿出去倒了，已經開始招來蒼蠅，臭死了。

2 形 優秀的、傑出的

"What do you think of the new movie?"

"It's **ripe**, and the special effects are cool!"

「你覺得那部新電影怎麼樣？」

「太讚了，特效超酷的！」

3 形 有點粗俗的、搞笑的

After a few drinks, Bernie started telling **ripe** jokes and got everyone laughing.

柏尼喝了杯後，開起黃腔，逗得大家笑呵呵。

ripe 最常見的用法應該是「發出臭味的」，這個用法源自英國，但通行於世界各地。如果你說有什麼聞起來很 ripe，大多是指東西，人也可以聞起來很 ripe，但你不會想待在附近。

如果你用 ripe 形容言語，表示聽起來搞笑，但有點粗俗。

rock [rɑk]

1 名 冰塊

Joe's favorite drink is a Jack and Coke on the **rocks**.

喬最喜歡喝的酒是傑克可樂加冰塊。

2 名 鑽石

When Jeff proposed to Amanda, he gave her the biggest **rock** she had ever seen.

傑夫跟阿曼達求婚時，送她一顆前所未見的大鑽石。

3 名 睪丸

There was a man getting fresh with Justina, so she kicked him in the **rocks**.

那男的騷擾賈絲汀娜，所以她踢了他的蛋蛋。

　　rock 是一個很好玩的字，最常用來表示「冰塊」。你點酒時酒保或服務生都會問你要 straight up（不加水、不加冰塊），還是要 on the rocks；此時 rock 會以複數型態出現。

　　雖然你可以用 rock 來指其他寶石，但當大家提到 rock 時，幾乎都是指「鑽石」。

　　如果你說話時不想裝文雅，也可用 rocks 表示「睪丸」；常見的說法為 kick him in the rocks（踢他的要害）。

rolling ['rolɪŋ]

1 〔形〕富有的

Brad built up a successful business, and now he's **rolling** in money.

布萊德的事業很成功，現在很富有。

2 〔形〕吸毒後的狀態

At the club the other night everyone was **rolling** on ecstasy.

前幾天晚上在夜店，每個人都嗑搖頭丸，嗑得飄飄欲仙。

let's roll

3 〔慣〕採取行動

If we're all ready, then **let's roll**. We need to be at the train station by nine.

都準備好了我們就出發吧！九點要到火車站。

　　這個字是最近 20 年左右興起的，其中以**rolling** 表示「賺大錢」的用法存在最久。如果真的很有錢，就可以在錢裡面打滾（roll）了，這樣想就不難記了。

　　搖頭丸的出現，為rolling 帶來新意，吃了搖頭丸的人都會描述飄飄欲仙的感覺，說他們正在 rolling。

　　Let's roll. 是在採取行動、發動攻擊之前會說的口號，意思是「我們上吧！」，展現出一種有決心的氣魄。準備好要做某件事之前，也可以這麼說。

rub down [rʌb]

1 名 搜身

Anytime you get pulled over for drinking and driving, the policeman will give you a **rub down**.

只要是酒駕被攔下來，警察都會搜身。

rub out

2 片 動 謀殺

The man paid a mobster to **rub out** his business partner. With his partner dead, he can collect the insurance money and become the company's sole owner.

這男的付錢請黑道把合夥人幹掉，合夥人死了他就可以領保險金，把公司佔為己有。

rub one out

3 片 動 打手槍

At the fertility clinic you have to **rub one out** in order to collect the sperm specimen.

在生育診所，你要打手槍才能收集精液樣本。

　　rub down（警察搜身）源自英國，也只在英國使用，在北美，rub down 稱作 strip search，搜查的程序是一樣的，如果你被警察攔了下來，他們會叫你雙手抱頭，兩腿張開。

　　用 **rub one out** 表示「手淫」，不是最普遍的說法，有點粗野。

run of the mill

1 慣 普通的、平常的

Libby was tired of dating **run of the mill** guys. She was looking for her prince to show up on his white horse and take her away.

麗比不想老跟平凡的男生約會,她期待王子騎著白馬出現帶她走。

run off one's mouth

2 慣 態度很差地說話

Georgia was **running off her mouth** to her teacher because she didn't want to do the work that he assigned. She felt he was being unfair.

喬治雅對老師出言不遜,因為她不想做老師分派給她的工作,她覺得老師不公平。

run-in

3 名 爭執、吵架

When Bill was in high school he would often have **run-ins** with the police. He always got himself into trouble.

比爾唸高中時常跟警察起爭執,老惹麻煩。

run around

4 慣 欺騙或逃避的回應

Kelly wanted to know her husband's whereabouts on Friday night after work. He kept giving her the **run around**. She knew something was up when he kept changing his story.

凱莉想知道老公星期五晚上下班後的行蹤，但老公言詞閃躲，說法不一，凱莉知道有鬼。

　　　　這幾個俚語都源自美國，在世界各地都普遍使用。若有人叫你stop **running off your mouth**（閉嘴），應該是你說話態度不佳，而對方大概是你的長輩。
　　run-in 表示與權威人士之間的「衝突」。
　　當你的伴侶不誠實、言詞閃躲，就是在 **run around**。

sack [sæk]

1 動 被開除

Rob got **sacked** last week. Now he's looking for a new job.
羅伯上星期被開除，現在在找新工作。

2 名 床

It's noon and Tom's still in the **sack**. 已經中午了湯姆還賴在床上。

sack out

3 片動 上床睡覺

The girls were so tired after a day at the beach that they **sacked out** in the car on the way home.
女孩們去海邊玩了一天，累壞了，回家時在車上全睡死了。

hit the sack

4 慣 睡覺

Let's **hit the sack**. I'm tired. 我們上床睡覺吧，我累了。

　　sack 原意「粗布大袋子」，當俚語 sack 有兩種用法「開除」和「睡覺」。每次有人被開除了，一定會用到這個字，在美國比較常用，但其他地方也會用。
　　hit the sack（上床睡覺），是很生動的説法，好像很累一頭栽在床上一樣。

164

salt away [ˈsɔlt əˈwe]

1

片動 存下

They **salted** the money **away** in many bank accounts around the world.

他們把錢存在世界各地好幾個帳戶。

salty [ˈsɔlti]

2

形 兇惡的、有侵略性的

Todd was a **salty** fellow who never let anyone push him around.

托德是個狠角色，從不任人擺佈。

take something with a grain of salt

3

慣 持保留態度

He's been wrong before, so I'll **take what he says with a grain of salt**.

他之前曾錯過，所以我對他說的話保留三分。

想要保存比較久的食物會用salt（鹽）醃過，因此**salt away**就衍生出「積存」的意思。

若你對某人說的話半信半疑，就可以說**take something with a grain/pinch of salt**，代表你持保留態度，不會全部採信。

scalp [skælp]

1 動 賣黃牛票以賺取暴利

Maria buys extra tickets for concerts so that she can **scalp** them right before the show and make money.

瑪麗亞多買了幾張演唱會的票,可以在表演前賣黃牛票賺一筆。

scalper

2 名 黃牛（賣黃牛票的人）

There are a lot of professional **scalpers**. Some sell concert tickets and others sell tickets for sporting events.

現在有好多專業的黃牛,有些賣演唱會的票,有些賣運動比賽的票。

在美國有一種專門賣黃牛票的人 scalper（專業黃牛）,他們跟售票人員打好關係,可以買到超過限額的票,位置也都非常好,當然票價也都很貴,但是你會買到最好的位置。

scene [sin]

1 名 某種活動的大環境

If you want to know what is hot on the fashion **scene** this month, just read *Vogue* or *Vanity Fair* magazine.

如果你想知道這個月時尚圈流行什麼，不妨看看《時尚》或《浮華世界》這些時尚雜誌。

make a scene

2 慣 當眾吵鬧

I know you're pissed off, but can you keep your voice down? You're **making a scene**. We'll talk about it when we get back home.

我知道你氣炸了，但你可以小聲點嗎？大家都在看你啦，我們回家再說。

　　scene 經常被想知道最新時尚的人使用，你可以透過報紙、雜誌、電視或網路找到最新的流行資訊，體會時尚圈大環境的氛圍。

　　如果有人 **make a scene**（當眾吵鬧），會引起旁人注意，讓場面變得很尷尬，你可以說：

Stop making such a scene!

別再丟人現眼了！

schizo ['skɪtso]

1 名 精神有問題的人

It is politically incorrect to call someone a **schizo** if they really do have a mental condition. This is a very serious disease.

如果有人真的有精神問題，你叫他們瘋子是不太對的，精神分裂是很嚴重的疾病。

schizzed out

2 形 瘋狂的

The prisoner was **schizzed out** from having been kept in solitary confinement for a month.

那犯人被獨立監禁了一個月以後，發瘋了。

    schizo 是 schizophrenic（患有精神分裂症的）的俚語説法，schizophrenia（精神分裂症）是一種精神疾病，病人的思想通常脱離現實，情緒、行為和心智都非常不穩定。

    schizo 最常用來開玩笑指稱那些有精神問題或能力缺失、但不一定患有精神分裂症的人，但是如果你用 schizo 來稱呼真的精神分裂症患者，非常不禮貌。

    schizzed out 源於美國，用來表示「瘋狂的」，源於 schizo。

schlub [ʃlʌb]

1 **名** 愚笨的人、枯燥乏味的人

Tina went on a blind date, but the guy she went out with turned out to be a **schlub**. She won't be seeing him again.

蒂娜參加聯誼，結果跟她出去的男生超笨的，她以後不想見他了。

schmo [ʃmo]

2 **名** 木訥呆滯的人

My last boyfriend was such a **schmo**. I could never get him interested in anything that I enjoyed doing.

我前男友真的很無聊，我根本沒辦法讓他喜歡我喜歡的事。

schmuck [ʃmʌk]

3 **名** 笨蛋

I often wonder how a **schmuck** like Allen could even graduate from college.

我常納悶為什麼像艾倫這麼笨的人也能大學畢業。

這三個俚語都源自美國，你也很少會有機會在美國以外的地區聽到這些說法，其中使用最普遍的是 **schmuck**，最常用的是：

Don't be such a schmuck. 別傻了。

這些字好玩的地方是，不是人人都聽過，但是多數人都能根據上下文一聽就懂。通常你也不須多加解釋，因為你可以簡單就看出 **schlub**、**schmo** 和 schmuck 之間的關聯！

schmooze　[ʃmuz]

1 動 討好、奉承

Dana was always **schmoozing** with her boss. She would buy her coffee and agree with everything she said.

戴娜老是在拍她老闆馬屁，幫她買咖啡，老闆說什麼她都同意。

2 名 為了好處善待他人

In order to climb to the top of the company, William had to do a lot of **schmoozing**.

為了爬上公司的最高層，威廉得打好人際關係，猛獻殷勤。

3 名 閒聊、八卦

The girls get together on Thursday nights for dinner and a bit of **schmoozing**.

女孩子們星期四晚上去聚餐、聊八卦。

　　schmooze 源於美國，常見的用法是「討好」和「為了利益而善待他人」。有些人覺得這兩個意義其實是相伴而來的，在討好對方時，基本上就是獻殷勤，好讓自己得到某些利益。

　　「討好」、「奉承」通常出現在工作場合，想要升官的下屬常會想盡辦法為上司做好所有事，以討好上司，像是拍馬屁、倒咖啡、跑腿、額外為上司做某些工作、上司說什麼都同意（即使心裡並不認同），或是損人來讓自己顯得更優秀等。

　　用 schmooze 表示「閒聊」、「八卦」也很常見，但是不如另外兩種用法普遍。

score [skor]

1 動 購買毒品

While on vacation, Adrian was able to **score** a bag of weed from one of the locals.

艾卓安去度假時，跟一個當地人買到一袋大麻。

2 動 打炮、上床

Todd spent the evening at the bar, looking to **score**.

托德晚上泡在酒吧裡，想找人打炮。

3 名 成功、勝利

Rachael landed the Manchester account on Friday afternoon. This was a big **score** for her; she has been working on this account for months.

瑞秋星期五下午終於爭取到曼徹斯特的客戶了，這對她來說可是一大勝利，她對這個客戶已經下了好幾個月的工夫了。

4 名 情況；現況

What's the **score**? Are they getting married?

現在情形怎樣？他們要結婚嗎？

know the score

5

慣 了解事情真相

Leo has been in the mob for years so he **knows the score**. If he rats out his partner and tells the police who killed the man, he'll be put away.

利歐在幫派裡混了好幾年,他知道所有事,如果他出賣他的同夥,跟警察說誰殺了那個人,他就會被幹掉。

　　score 普遍用於世界各地,其五種意義都使用得相當頻繁,至於說話者會使用哪種用法,就視他們的年齡和個性了。例如青少年、大學生、二三十歲的人多用 score 表示「打炮」或「購買毒品」。

　　商界人士多用 score 談及他們的工作、家庭或嗜好。

　　當你搞不清楚發生了什麼事,特別是原定計畫已經被打亂時,你就可以問 What's the score? 來搞清楚現在的狀況。

171

screw [skru]

1 動 私通、性交

Have you heard? Andy is **screwing** Carl's girlfriend!

你聽説了嗎？安迪搞上了卡爾的女朋友。

screw over

2 片 動 佔便宜、不公平地對待

Monica's boss was always **screwing** her **over** because he knew that she needed this job more than he needed her.

莫妮卡的老闆老是壓榨她，因為他知道莫妮卡很需要這份工作，老闆卻不一定需要她。

screw around

3 片 動 瞎混

Bruce and Amy, please stop **screwing around** and finish your work.

布魯斯、艾咪，別混了，快把功課做完。

4 片 動 亂搞男女關係

You should really stop **screwing around**, settle down, and get married. You're not a kid anymore; be a man.

你不要再亂搞了，安定下來，結婚吧！你已經不是小孩了，當個男子漢吧！

screw someone around

5 ⑱ 因為猶豫不決，造成別人的麻煩

Jenny kept **screwing us around**, telling us that she would move in to the apartment the following week but never showing up. In the end, she screwed up our May rent.

珍妮一直把我們耍得團團轉，説下星期要搬進公寓，結果都沒出現，害我們浪費五月的房租。

　　screw 指「性交」，很粗俗的説法，通常是指情侶以外的性行為。

　　screw around 就是「亂搞男女關係」; screw around 也表「瞎混」、「遊手好閒」。

　　screw someone around 意「擺某人一道」，某人因猶豫不決讓計畫泡湯時，可以這麼説。

screw up

1 片動 毀壞、搞砸事情

She had the perfect night planned for her boyfriend's birthday, but it rained and screwed up everything!

她為男友生日計畫了一個完美的夜晚，但是下雨把一切都搞砸了！

2 片動 使人精神受創

Emma was pretty screwed up after she witnessed someone get hit by a train on her way to work.

艾瑪在上班途中目睹一個人被火車撞到，心裡受到很大的創傷。

screw up one's courage

3 慣 鼓起勇氣

Stacy screwed up her courage and confessed that she didn't finish her homework.

史黛西鼓起勇氣，承認她沒做完功課。

have a screw loose

4 慣 有點發瘋的

All those years of fighting in the military have caused him to have a few screws loose.

這幾年來在軍隊打仗讓他心理不太正常。

screwball

5 名 古怪的人

Geoff seemed like a normal guy during the job interview, but he turned out to be a real screwball when he started working for us.

傑弗面試時看起來很正常，他開始上班後卻變成怪咖。

screw up 很常用，表示「搞砸」或「精神受創」。

screw up one's courage 或 screw up one's nerve 表示你得做好心理準備，才能去完成某件困難的事。

　　身體像是用螺絲釘（screw）組裝起來的，如果有螺絲釘鬆掉，就表示身體出了問題，而鬆掉的那根剛好就是固定腦袋的，所以 have a screw loose 用來指「發瘋」。

　　在上述俚語中，screwball（怪人）是最少用的。

screw you

1 嘆 罵人的話，類似滾開或去你的

"Hey, Erin, you're getting fat. You should really go on a diet."

"Screw you. Have you looked in the mirror lately?"

「嘿，艾琳，你最近胖了，真該減減肥了。」

「去你的！那你最近照過鏡子沒有？」

screwed

2 形 喝醉的

Daniela got pretty screwed at her going away party. She couldn't even make it to the after-hours club she had planned to go to.

丹妮葉拉在她的餞行派對上喝得爛醉，根本沒辦法再去原本要續攤的酒吧。

　　screw you（去你的）是一個相當普遍、又不會太過粗野的罵法，它跟 fuck you 一樣，但是又不會讓人覺得是髒話。
　　screwed 表示「喝醉」，來自於英國，常用於當事人本身不想喝這麼醉的時候。

screwy ['skruɪ]

1

形 瘋狂的、古怪的

What is wrong with you? Are you **screwy**? I would never do something like that behind your back!

你怎麼搞的？你瘋了嗎？我絕對不會背著你做那種事！

2

形 荒謬的

There's something **screwy** about this situation. No way would Matthew ever say that about his roommate.

這情況也太誇張了，馬修絕不會這樣說他室友的。

screw 原意「擰、轉（螺絲釘）」，和 **screwy**（瘋狂的、古怪的）有點關聯，這些人想法與常人不同，會彎來彎去的，而這也是 screwy 最常見的用法。

其次常用的是「荒謬的」，它與原意的關聯就與「瘋狂的」、「古怪的」類似。

scum [skʌm]

1 名 沒有價值的人

That politician is **scum**! He's gotten rich from the taxpayers' money and has made no contributions to society.

那個政客真是個人渣！他污了納稅人的錢，又對社會毫無貢獻。

scum-sucker

2 名 令人不屑的小人

Robert is a **scum-sucker**. He is rude to everyone and thinks only of himself.

羅柏特真令人不恥，他對每個人都很無禮，只想到自己。

scum-sucking

3 形 噁心的

That **scum-sucking** man just raced in front of an old lady and sat down in a seat reserved for elderly people. Luckily, someone else gave up his seat for her, so she didn't have to remain standing for long.

那個噁心男人剛跑在老太太前搶坐博愛座，幸好有人讓位給老太太，她才不用站那麼久。

scumbag [ˋskʌmˌbæg]

4 名 卑鄙小人

Greg is such a **scumbag**. He cheats on both his wife and his mistress.

葛瑞格真是卑鄙小人，他對老婆和小三都不忠。

scumwad [ˋskʌmˌwɑd]

5 名 低級庸俗的人

Do you see that **scumwad** over there? He came over to me and told me I was "hot;" then he asked me out on a date.

你有沒有看到那邊那個低級男人？他剛走過來跟我說我很「辣」，還想約我出去。

　　上面這幾個用來罵人的俚語都源自美國。scum 原來是「液體表面薄薄的一層浮渣」，用「浮垢」、「渣滓」來形容人真的很狠毒。

　　scumwad 和 scumbag 的意思相同，但後者比較常用。scum-sucker 和 scum-sucking 都不算髒話，但也不是什麼好聽的話，不太常用，用 scum 就能達到同樣的效果，也比較沒那麼難聽。

scuzz [skʌz]

1 名 令人噁心反感的人

When I think of all the **scuzzes** at the bars on Saturday night, it makes me wonder where all the good men are.

每當我想起星期六晚上酒吧裡的那些噁心男人，我就在想好男人都到哪兒去了。

scuzzed out

2 形 感到噁心

He was **scuzzed out** by the sight of the puddle of vomit on the sidewalk.

他看到人行道上有一灘嘔吐物，覺得很噁。

scuzzy [ˈskʌzi]

3 形 骯髒的

I refuse to stay at this **scuzzy** hotel, regardless of how cheap it is. I wouldn't want my cat to sleep in that rank room.

我不想待在這間髒旅館，不管它有多便宜，我才不要讓我的貓睡在那種房間。

　　骯髒的東西和噁心的人都可以被稱為 **scuzz**，或用 **scuzzy** 來形容。今天我們還是會使用這幾個字，但較不普遍。最愛說這個字的通常是青少年，**scuzzy** 比另外兩個字還常用。

seedy ['sidɪ]

1

形 破舊骯髒的（地方）

The apartment my friends moved into was pretty seedy. It was in a poor neighborhood and everything seemed to be falling apart.

我朋友搬進去住的那間公寓非常破，它位在一個很差的社區裡，所有東西好像都快解體了。

2

形 穿著破舊邋遢

The homeless man wore seedy clothes and had dirt under his fingernails.

那流浪漢穿得很破爛，指甲裡都是汙泥。

3

形 風評不好的、聲名狼藉的

The diner that my friend Todd took me to was a seedy hole-in-the-wall kind of place, but the food was good.

我朋友托德帶我去一家風評不好的餐館，又小又不起眼，不過東西滿好吃的。

seedy 表示「看起來破舊、骯髒」，住在這種地方的人往往也穿得很破舊邋遢。不是所有看起來 seedy 的地方都不適合去，有時候，最好的食物或最好的酒，就是在這些沒錢搬到好地段，或是沒錢整修的餐廳或酒吧才找得到。

seedy 也可以表示「名聲不好的」，a seedy lawyer，就是指聲名狼藉的律師。

sexpert [ˋsɛkspɚt]

1

名 性專家

I'm not a **sexpert**, but I'd like to think I know what turns a man on.

我不是性專家，但是我想我知道怎樣可以讓男人興奮。

sexpot [ˋsɛks‚pɑt]

2

名 性感尤物

Marilyn Monroe was considered a real **sexpot** back in the fifties and sixties.

瑪麗蓮‧夢露是五〇、六〇年代公認的性感尤物。

　　這兩個字都是從 sex 衍生而來的。把 sex 和 expert 這兩個字合在一起，就會變成 **sexpert**，有點文字遊戲的意味。如果你對性很了解，或是你覺得你很了解，那你可能就會自認為是個性專家（sexpert），這個字比較不常用，如果用了也多是在開玩笑。

　　sexpot 指「性感尤物」，通常男人會視她為可隨便上勾的、生活淫亂的年輕女性。

shack [ʃæk]

1 图 小房子或小商店

My grandfather made his great-grandchildren a **shack** for them to play in. It had windows with curtains, a table and chairs, and a fake fireplace.

我爺爺為他的曾孫們蓋了一間小屋，讓他們在裡面玩，小屋有窗戶、窗簾、桌子、椅子和一個假的壁爐。

shack up

2 片 動 和人上床，多為一夜情

When my roommate didn't come home last night, I knew he must have **shacked up** with someone at the party.

我室友昨晚沒回來，我猜他一定是和派對上某個人搞一夜情了。

3 片 動 同居

Michelle and Bill have been **shacking up** for almost five years. They may as well be married.

米雪兒和比爾同居將近五年了，他們其實跟結婚差不多了。

多數人看到 **shack**，第一個想到的都是「小房子」或「小商店」。shack 可指用來放除草機或是節日裝飾用品的小房子，也可以指小孩的遊戲屋，跟樹屋差不多，只是 shack 是建在地上的。

大學生和那些經常出沒酒吧找一夜情的人最常用 **shack up** 了，年輕人之間很常用這個指「上床」。

shades [ʃedz]

1 **名** 太陽眼鏡

Has anyone seen my **shades**? I am going to the beach and I will definitely need them.

有人看到我的太陽眼鏡嗎？我要去海邊，一定要有太陽眼鏡。

shady [ˈʃedɪ]

2 **形** 腐敗的、不法的

In the world of politics, many **shady** deals take place behind closed doors.

在政治圈，許多見不得人的交易都秘密進行。

3 **形** 鬼鬼祟祟、不可信賴的人

The new employee you hired seems a bit **shady**. I would keep an eye on him if I were you.

你請的新人好像有點不老實，如果我是你，我會好好盯著他。

　　shades（太陽眼鏡）用於北美地區；英國、澳洲、南非、紐西蘭用 sunnies 表示「太陽眼鏡」。

　　shady 源於美國，「貪污、不法的」形容事物；「不誠實」形容人。跟貪污扯上關係的人通常就是不誠實的人，兩個詞義雖不同，但多少有點關聯。

shaft [ʃæft]

1 名 陰莖

Men sometimes use the word "shaft" to refer to their penis.

男人有時會用「小弟弟」來稱呼陰莖。

shafted

2 形 被戲弄、被欺騙

Samantha got shafted by the car salesman. He sold her a lemon.

莎曼珊被汽車業務騙了，他賣她一部爛車。

get the shaft

3 慣 嚴厲、不公平、殘酷的待遇

Factory workers continue to get the shaft with minimum wage while the big bosses get rich.

工廠工人持續受到不平的對待，領最低工資，大老闆卻越來越富有。

shaft 最常用來指「不公平或嚴厲的懲罰」，談及這樣的懲罰時，shaft 和 shafted 兩個字皆可使用。I got shafted.（我被整得很慘。）或 You got shafted.（你被整得很慘。）是最常聽到的。

這個字雖然指的是「嚴厲的懲罰」，但多是朋友間描述自己受到不公平待遇時才使用，像是在一群人當中偏偏就是你要去商店買東西。

用 shaft 和 shafted 表示「被戲弄」、「被欺騙」的用法也很普遍，說話者的口吻通常都是輕鬆愉快的。

shag [ʃæg]

1 動 做愛

On Wednesday, Lucy went to her ex-boyfriend's house to pick up a book and they ended up **shagging**.

露西星期三去前男友家拿書，結果兩個人上床了。

shagged out

2 片動 累壞了

I'm all **shagged out**; I've been studying all night.

唸了一整晚的書，我實在累壞了。

shagnasty

3 名 噁心的男人

That guy is a **shagnasty**! I wouldn't be around him if I were you.

那男的很噁心，如果我是你，我不會靠近他。

　　這幾個字都源於英國，雖然英語世界國家都知道 **shag**，但是英國以外的人通常不太用。當你不想露骨地說 Do you want to have sex with me?（你想跟我上床嗎？），shag 就是一個很好用的字。

　　用 **shagged** 表示「精疲力竭」，通常後面會接 out。

shark [ʃɑrk]

1 图 非常有能力、非常聰明的學生

Some of my advanced English students are real **sharks**! It's amazing how gifted they are at such a young age.

我有些英語進階班的學生真的很聰明！他們才這麼小就這麼厲害，真不可思議。

card shark

2 图 會記牌、算牌的賭徒

In the casinos in Las Vegas, you'll find many **card sharks** that are hoping to win big!

在拉斯維加斯的賭場裡，你會看到很多老千想大贏一筆！

loan shark

3 图 放高利貸的人

Albert was desperate for money to pay off his gambling debts so he went to a **loan shark**.

艾伯特為了還賭債走投無路，只好去找放高利貸的人。

shark 表示「非常有能力、非常聰明的學生」，源自美國。

card shark 是指玩撲克牌會記牌、算牌的專業賭徒，就是老千，若是出老千被抓到，下場很慘的。

而 **loan shark** 是指放高利貸的人，他們借錢給人，收取很高的利息。

schlep [ʃlɛp]

1 動 拖、拉、扛東西

Lyle **schlepped** all his belongings from his old apartment to his new one in five separate carloads.

萊爾開了五趟車,把他所有的家當從舊家搬到新家了。

2 動 吃力地前進

Linda had to **schlep** from one end of the airport to the other just to take the train that would take her to her hotel.

琳達得拖著笨重的行李橫越整個機場,這樣才能搭到飯店的火車。

3 名 冗長乏味或令人疲倦的旅程

Backpacking for six months across Asia was a long **schlep** that I'm glad I did, but I wouldn't want to do it again anytime soon.

在亞洲背包旅行六個月真是漫長,我很高興我這麼做,但近期內我絕對不想再來一次。

schlepper

4 图 笨手笨腳的人、拖拖拉拉的人

The woman I work with, Sarah, is a **schlepper**. She's always asking me to do things for her the minute I'm about to leave for the day.

我同事莎拉真是笨手笨腳，每次都在我準備下班的時候，請我幫她做這做那的。

Don't be such a **schlepper**. Just make a list of everything you need to do today and get it done!

不要再拖拖拉拉的，把你今天要做的事列張清單，趕快做一做！

　　北美地區的猶太人經常使用 **schlep**（動詞）來表示「拖、拉或扛抬重物」。

　　schlep 其次常用的意義為「吃力地前進」，還會令人想到「漫長而辛苦的旅程」，因旅客常要拖著或扛著重物，所以一再被耽擱。

　　下次你有什麼沉重的負荷必須背負時，schlep 就可以用來描述你遇到的困難。

　　schlep（名詞）或 **schlepper** 也可以指「笨拙、動作很慢的人」。

shit [ʃɪt]

1 名 屎

He hated to change his son's diapers because he couldn't stand the smell of **shit**.

他最討厭幫兒子換尿布了，因為他沒辦法忍受便便的味道。

2 動 大便、拉屎

Kylie loved to go camping, but she hated **shitting** in the woods.

凱莉很想去露營，但是她討厭在樹林裡拉屎。

3 名 胡說、廢話

You are so full of **shit**. That never happened!

你亂講，從來沒發生過這種事！

4 名 自私、卑劣、可惡的人

Alex treated Julia like **shit** by calling off their wedding at the last minute. If he had had second thoughts about marriage, he could at least have had the respect to talk to her about it.

艾力克斯對茱莉亞很差勁，在最後一刻取消婚禮，如果他想改變心意，至少要尊重茱莉亞，跟她談一談。

5 嘆 表示厭惡、惱怒等

Shit! I think I left my cell phone in the restaurant. Now I have to drive all the way back to get it.

媽的！我手機忘在餐廳了，現在要再開回去拿。

6 名 極好的、棒透的

Wow! That new album you have is the **shit**!

哇！你買的那張新專輯實在酷斃了！

7 動 戲弄或欺騙

"Did you know that Kyle won the lottery?"

"You're **shitting** me, right?"

"Nope, I **shit** you not."

「你知道凱爾中了樂透嗎？」

「你開玩笑的吧？」

「不，我沒開玩笑。」

shits

8 名 拉肚子

After eating all that spicy Indian curry, Miguel got the **shits**.

吃那麼多辣的印度咖哩，麥基最後落賽了。

give a shit

9 慣 在乎

Debby's ex will be at the party with his new girlfriend, but she doesn't **give a shit**.

黛比的前夫會帶新歡去派對，但黛比才不鳥他。

shit 永遠不會退流行，它有好幾種用法，而且都用得很頻繁。多數人會覺得 shit 是髒話，所以不會在小孩子或是他們覺得會冒犯到的人面前說這個字。

當shit 表示「大便」的常用句：

I took a shit. 我剛嗯嗯。
I have to shit. 我要去便便。
I can't shit. 我大不出來。

如果把 shit 當髒話說，表示「胡說」、「亂講」，通常會說 bullshit（亂講）或You are full of shit.（你亂講。），而不會單獨說 shit。

如果用 shit 表示「自私、卑劣、可惡的人」，通常會說 You're a piece of shit.（你這個爛人。）。

最近出現的新用法則是用shit表示「極好的」、「讚透的」。你經常可以聽到高中生、大學生、二三十歲的人說：

That is the shit. 棒呆了。

shit a brick

1 慣 嚇到

He nearly **shit a brick** when he walked into his bedroom and saw a spider bigger than his hand crawling up his wall.

他走進臥室看到一隻比他手還大的蜘蛛在牆上爬時,真的被嚇壞了。

shit oneself

2 慣 嚇得屁滾尿流

The movie that Paul watched the other day was so scary that he nearly **shit himself**. It was very graphic.

保羅前幾天看的那部電影實在太恐怖了,他差點嚇到挫賽,電影好寫實。

scared shitless

3 慣 極度驚恐、嚇得半死

Nora was **scared shitless** when two huge men cornered her as she was walking back to her hostel. She kicked one in the nuts and ran away.

諾拉走回青年旅社時,被兩個大男人逼到角落,把她嚇死了。她踢了一個人的蛋蛋後就跑掉了。

shit one's pants

4 慣 嚇到挫賽

Mary **shit her pants** when she was stopped at the customs desk crossing the border into Canada. She was carrying drugs on her, and she was afraid they'd find them.

瑪麗進入加拿大的邊境時,在海關櫃檯被攔了下來,嚇到挫賽。她身上帶有毒品,她很怕被海關發現。

　　只要有什麼東西或什麼事情讓你嚇得半死,嚇到你覺得自己真的會屁滾尿流時,你就可以使用這幾個俚語。

　　對某些人來說,可能是看到某種昆蟲、恐怖電影,或是見到某人或某樣東西,這時覺得自己快要 scared shitless(嚇到魂不附體),就要 shit oneself(挫賽)或 shit one's pants(挫賽),或是更常聽到 shit a brick(挫賽)。

　　不過,當事者在事後講起這段經歷時,通常是挺好笑的,而且他們往往會用上面這幾個字描述受到驚嚇後的反應。

shit on

1 片動 欺負、打壓

Quentin **shits on** his employees every chance he gets. For example, he made Leah work overtime last week to do research and write up a report for the conference, and then he took credit for her work.

昆汀每次一有機會就欺壓員工，例如，他上週叫莉亞加班、做研究、寫研討會的報告，然後功勞都歸給自己。

shit or get off the pot

2 價 別占著茅坑不拉屎

Jack's not sure yet if he'll take the job, but he needs to **shit or get off the pot** because there are dozens of other people who would jump at the chance to get that position.

傑克還不確定他想不想要這份工作，但他得決定，不能占著茅坑不拉屎，因為還有一群人急著想做這份工作。

shit on（欺負、打壓），可以 shit on someone，也可以 be shit on，不管是主動或被動，都不是好事。

shit or get off the pot 是個絕不會過時的俚語，意思很接近中文的「占著茅坑，不拉屎，要上就趕快上」，只要有人猶豫不決，就可以這麼跟他說，是很生動的說法。

shithead

1 名 可惡的人

Rob is trying to make Carla look like a schlep in front of the boss so that he can get the promotion instead of her. He's such a shithead.

羅伯想讓卡拉在老闆面前像個笨蛋，這樣他就可以打敗她而升職，真是壞心眼。

shitbag

2 名 可憎、可鄙的人

Look, you shitbag! If you touch me again, I'm going to call the police.

王八蛋！如果你再碰我，我就要叫警察了。

shit for brains

3 慣 特別笨的人

Nick has shit for brains. I don't understand how Leslie can date a man that dumb!

尼克腦袋只裝屎，我真不懂萊絲莉怎麼會跟一個這麼蠢的人在一起！

沒有人願意被稱為 shit（屎），不過如果你煩到別人，或是你不用大腦，那你可能就會被冠上這些稱號了。

這幾個字雖然大多都含有負面意義，有時候朋友間還是會開玩笑地稱呼彼此 shithead 或 shit for brains，可以達意，但是不會觸怒對方。

shitfaced

1 形 喝得很醉

Joe and I had too much to drink last night and got totally **shitfaced**. 阿喬和我昨晚喝太多，喝掛了。

shithole

2 名 髒到令人無法忍受的地方

The hostel that we stayed in while we were in Hungary was a total **shithole**. The bathroom was scuzzy, and I was afraid to even put my head on the pillow. 我們在匈牙利住的青年旅社髒透了，廁所髒得讓我受不了，還有我根本不敢把頭靠在枕頭上。

on someone's shitlist

3 慣 黑名單

Believe me, you don't want to get **on Maria's shitlist**. If she finds out that you lied to her, she'll make your life miserable.

相信我，你不會想被瑪利亞列入黑名單，如果她發現你說謊，她會讓你過得很慘。

年輕人最常說 shitfaced（爛醉如泥）和 shithole（骯髒的地方），可能因為年輕人離家後住的公寓往往就是個 shithole！一旦他們離開了這個 shithole，得到一份真正的工作後，就得小心不要被開除或是被列入 shitlist 了，被列入黑名單，會對你的事業造成很大的影響，應極力避免。

shoot

1 嘆 表示厭惡、惱怒等

Shoot! I left my keys inside the car, and I locked the door.
可惡！我把鑰匙鎖在車上了。

2 動 說吧；問吧

"Do you mind if I ask you a personal question?"
"Not at all. **Shoot**."
「你介意我問你私人問題嗎？」
「一點也不，問吧！」

shoot up

3 片 動 注射海洛因

Junkies sometimes come to this alley to **shoot up**.
毒蟲有時會來這條巷子，打海洛因。

　　shoot 是表示厭惡、惱怒等情緒的感嘆語，用於北美地區，女生覺得說 shit 有損形象，因此改說 shoot，聽起來較委婉，也不會冒犯別人。

　　shoot 原意為「開槍射傷或射死」，也有「發射（槍砲）」或「迅速排出」的意思。了解這點以後，你就可以看出原意和 shoot up 之間的關聯了。

　　海洛因通常以固體形式販賣，所以要先把海洛因加熱，熔成液體，放進針筒打進手臂的靜脈裡，因此打海洛因的人最常用 **shoot up**（注射毒品）。

shoot the breeze

1 慣 閒聊

Janelle, Magda, Olga, and Lily **shot the breeze** over dinner.

珍妮爾、瑪格達、奧加和麗麗一邊吃晚餐，一邊閒聊。

shoot the bull

2 慣 閒聊

The guys at the bar were watching the game intently, but when the commercials were on, they would **shoot the bull**.

酒吧裡的男人緊盯比賽，廣告一來就閒聊了起來。

shoot the shit

3 慣 閒聊、八卦

Every time I call Nora back in Canada I would **shoot the shit** with her for hours, filling her in on everything that has been happening here.

每次我打電話到加拿大給諾拉，都會跟她聊上好幾個小時，把這裡發生的大小八卦都告訴她。

4 慣 說大話、誇張

Don't pay too much attention to what he's saying; he's just **shooting the shit**.

不用太注意聽他說的話，他只是愛說大話。

shoot one's mouth off

(慣) 口無遮攔

Andrea would always **shoot her mouth off** to her mother when she didn't like the rules her mother set for her.

每次安卓雅不爽她媽定的規矩，就會跟媽媽講話沒大沒小。

(慣) 自誇

Nathan was **shooting his mouth off** about how he received a perfect score on his exam and how the professor wants him to be his assistant next semester.

納森吹牛說他考試考得有多好，還有教授多希望他下學期去當他的助理。

　　shoot的原意「發射」和這些片語正好直接相關，這四個片語都跟說話有關。

　　shoot the bull、**shoot the breeze**和**shoot the shit**都可指「隨意聊天」。shoot the shit還有「說大話」的意思。

　　shoot one's mouth off有兩個意思，一是「口無遮攔」，說話沒有顧忌；二是「自誇」，讓人覺得很煩。

192

shot [ʃɑt]

1 形 **精疲力竭的**

I'm **shot**. I didn't come home till really late last night, and then I hung out with my roommates till sunrise.

我累斃了，我昨天晚上好晚才回到家，然後又跟朋友出去玩到天亮。

2 形 **喝醉的**

Mel was really upset when he got fired, so he went to a bar and got totally **shot**.

梅爾被炒魷魚很難過，他去酒吧把自己灌醉。

3 形 **壞掉、故障**

My stereo speakers are completely **shot**. I have to buy new ones.

我的音響喇叭完全壞掉了，我得買新的了。

take a shot at something

4 片 動 **嘗試**

You will never know if you can do it unless you **take a shot at it**!

不試試看，你永遠也不知道你會不會成功。

shot 表示「精疲力竭的」和 shoot 的動詞用法並無直接關聯，下次當你累到頭抬不起來、眼睛也睜不開的時候，你就可以説 I'm shot.。

have/take a shot at something 表示「嘗試某事」，是一個很常見的片語，必學。

shove it

1 慣 告訴對方你實在沒興趣聽他們說話

Listen, Allen, I think you are full of shit so why don't you just shove it! I have nothing more to say to you.

艾倫，你聽著，我覺得你滿嘴廢話，你閉嘴吧！我不想再跟你說了。

shove off

2 片 動 離開

"Hey, shove off. You've had enough to drink and you're bothering the other customers," the bartender said to the man.

酒保跟那男的說：「嘿，走吧，你已經喝夠多了，你打擾到其他客人了。」

　　這兩個俚語都和 shove 的原意有關。shove 是「推」、「撞」的意思，有時候是個相當無禮的動作。

　　如果你對別人說 shove it，代表你有點生氣，不想聽對方說話，雖然這聽起來有些直接，但事實上這還算是比較客氣的說法。

　　shove off 的意思也很類似，「叫對方走開」。你可用肢體語言代替直接說出 shove off，把手放在胸前，然後再往旁邊一甩。這是「請你離開」的國際語言。

shtick [ʃtɪk]

1 名 喜劇諧星的滑稽場面或拿手好戲

The comedian's **shtick** is making fun of celebrities and politicians. It always gets the audience laughing.

這喜劇演員的拿手好戲就是調侃名流和政客，逗得觀眾哈哈大笑。

2 名 特殊才能

Telling people what they want to hear isn't my **shtick**. I prefer to be honest most of the time.

講別人愛聽的話不是我的專長，我大多喜歡誠實。

Chris has this **shtick** that he only uses when he meets new people. It's so tiresome to see him say and do the same thing over and over again.

克里斯出門認識新朋友時就會這樣，看他這樣老是說同樣的話、做同樣的動作，實在很膩。

這兩個意義有點相近，最常用的是「喜劇演員的拿手好戲」。一個人有 shtick，就表示他有自己的特色或者有什麼特殊才能。

skank [skæŋk]

1

名 骯髒的人

What a **skank**. He smells like he hasn't taken a shower in a week.

真是個髒鬼。他聞起來好像一個禮拜沒洗澡了！

2

名 賤人；蕩婦

Everyone's glad that Todd finally broke up with that **skank** Lisa.

大家都很高興，托德終於跟那個賤貨麗莎分手了。

skanky [ˈskæŋkɪ]

3

形 骯髒的

That is the **skankiest** part of town I've walked through. There was garbage everywhere on the streets.

那真是我走過城裡最髒亂的地帶了，街上到處是垃圾。

4

形 淫蕩的；隨便的

I didn't try to score with any of the girls at the bar last night. They were all a bit **skanky**.

我才不想跟昨晚酒吧裡的任何女孩上床，她們全都有點隨便。

skank 源自美國，可指骯髒的人。多是年輕的一代在說。
如果你用 **skanky** 形容女生，那表示這個女生不只隨便，
而且還看起髒髒的。這個字偶爾也用來形容男生，但還是多
用來形容女生。

S

196

skeeter [ˋskitɚ]

1 图 蚊子

The **skeeters** are so bad in the summer that you can't leave the house without bug spray.

夏天的蚊子實在很兇猛,所以出門絕對不能不噴防蚊液。

2 图 小胸部

Some women wear push-up bras because they want to make their **skeeters** look bigger.

有些女人會穿有厚墊的內衣,把胸部擠上來,因為她們想讓小奶看起來比較大。

　　skeeter是從mosquito的發音取出來的字,兩個俚語用法都源於北美,它最常用來指「蚊子」。

　　「小小的胸部」被稱為skeeter的原因也和「蚊子」有關,我們被蚊子叮咬後,皮膚上常起一個小小的包,如果我們用skeeter描述女生的胸部,就表示該女生的胸部跟蚊子叮的包一樣小,這個形容很誇張,又很生動,但對女生來說,可是很不禮貌的。

slag [slæg]

1 名 妓女或淫亂的女生

That **slag** slept with three different guys this week, and it's only Tuesday.

今天也不過星期二，那個浪女就已經跟三個人上床了。

2 名 可鄙的男人

Phil lied to Nadine by telling her that his parents had died and that his fiancée killed herself two weeks before their wedding. What kind of **slag** would say such things?

菲爾騙娜汀說他爸媽都過世了，而他未婚妻在婚禮舉行前的兩個星期自殺了，什麼樣的爛人會說這種話？

這兩個用法都源於英國，很少在英國以外的地區使用。
slag 最常用來指「性生活淫亂的女人」，上述用法都有貶義。

slag someone off

1 片動 以羞辱的方式批評

Don't start **slagging me off**; you're the one acting like an idiot!
你別批評我，你才像白痴呢！
Marina's constantly **slagging her friends off** behind their backs.
瑪莉一直在朋友背後講他們的八卦。

slag down

2 片動 口頭斥責

Jack's teachers are always **slagging** him **down** for getting into trouble.
傑克的老師老是罵他愛惹麻煩。

slagger

3 名 評論家

The restaurant **slagger** gave a nasty review of Fred's restaurant, saying that it'll probably go out of business by the end of the year.
美食評論家給弗萊德的餐廳下了一個很爛的評論，說它大概年底就會關門大吉了。

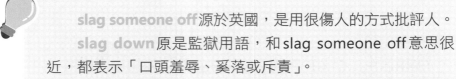

slag someone off 源於英國，是用很傷人的方式批評人。
slag down 原是監獄用語，和 slag someone off 意思很近，都表示「口頭羞辱、奚落或斥責」。
slagger（評論家）源於英國，他們的工作就是去鑑賞食物、音樂或電影，同時做出評論。

slam [slæm]

1 動 嚴苛的批評或辱罵

The athlete was **slammed** by newspapers for taking performance-enhancing drugs.

該運動員服用禁藥，受到報紙猛烈抨擊。

2 動 很快地把酒喝光

Before going on stage to perform with his band, Keith **slammed** down a shot of whisky. 基思上台跟他的樂團表演前灌了一杯威士忌。

slammed

3 形 喝醉的

Lyle got so **slammed** at the party that he couldn't even make it back to his dorm room. 萊爾在派對上喝掛了，甚至醉到走不回宿舍。

slammer ['slæmɚ]

4 名 監獄

The man was put in the **slammer** for drug possession.

那男的因為持有毒品被關進監獄裡。

slam 有兩個俚語用法，一為「羞辱或批評」；二為「灌酒」，皆源於北美，英國人則用 slammed 表示「喝醉的」。

大多數英語國家都知道 slammer 是「監獄」，牢房的門被用力一關（slam），犯人從此失去自由。

sleaze [sliz]

1 名 爛貨；骯髒；汙穢

A bunch of us were out the other night, and we saw this girl hitting on Rebecca's boyfriend. What a total **sleaze** she was.

前幾天晚上我們一群人一起出去，結果有個女的勾引瑞貝卡的男友，真是個爛人！

Al had always wanted to be a film actor, but he didn't realize how much **sleaze** went on in the movie business until he arrived in Hollywood.

艾爾一直想當電影演員，但他到了好萊塢才知道電影業有許多上不了枱面的齷齪事。

sleazebag/sleazeball

2 名 賤人；爛人

What a **sleazebag**! He grabbed the waitress's bottom when she was serving him his food.

超賤的！女服務生上菜時，他居然摸人家的屁股。

Some of the boys in my neighborhood can be such **sleazeballs**. They'd stand on the corner and make obscene comments to girls as they walked by.

我們社區有些男孩超爛的，他們會站在街角，對路過的女孩說一些猥褻的話。

sleazebucket

3 名 可鄙的人

Sally went on a blind date with a huge **sleazebucket** on Friday night. He took her out to dinner then told her that she "owed" him something since he paid for the meal!

莎莉星期五晚上跟一個大混球相親，他帶她去吃晚餐，吃完後居然跟她說她「欠」他一點東西，因為晚餐錢是他付的！

sleazy

4 形 破舊邋遢的

The bar where Mia worked was kind of **sleazy**. She hated working there, but the money was good.

米雅工作的那間酒吧有點破，她很不喜歡在那裡工作，不過薪水還不錯。

　　這幾個字都很好玩，而且可以互換使用，世界上有很多人符合它們的定義，這些字已經出現很久了，它們不算最狠的用語，但是依然能夠達到罵人的效果，大多時候，我們並不會用這些字直接罵人，而多是在事後跟別人描述時才會用到。

slime [slaɪm]

1 名 可憎的人

You are a **slime**! You don't know when to stop, do you?

你這個討厭鬼！你不懂什麼叫適可而止吧？

slimebag

2 名 不尊重他人的人

The taxi driver was a total **slimebag**. He was rude the minute we got in the cab, and then he ended up overcharging us.

那計程車司機真討厭，我們一上車他就很不客氣，後來還多收我們錢。

slimeball

3 名 令人厭惡的人

Todd was a **slimeball**. He slept with his girlfriend's roommate.

陶德真是個爛人，竟然跟他女友的室友上床。

slimebucket

4 名 卑鄙下流的人

Lisa had dated her fair share of **slimebuckets**. I was so happy she finally found someone nice.

麗莎遇到的爛人已經夠多了，我真高興她終於找到了一個好男人。

slime（討厭鬼）是名詞，而 slimy 是形容詞，加強語氣形容某人討厭的為人或行為。

smack [smæk]

1 名 海洛因

Oren got caught for trafficking **smack** and was thrown in the slammer for 12 years.

歐倫因走私海洛因被補，被關了 12 年。

smack off

2 片 動 打手槍

I hope I never walk in on my little brother **smacking off**. That would be awkward!

我希望再也不要撞見弟弟打手槍，超尷尬的！

smack out

3 片 動 吸海洛因吸得很嗨

If you look around in some of the parks in the seedy sections of town, you'll find lots of people **smacked out** on the benches.

如果你去鎮上貧民區的公園裡看看，就會看到很多人在長椅上吸毒吸得很嗨。

smacker [ˋsmækɚ]

4 名 大聲的吻

Before Pete got on the train, he turned around and planted a **smacker** right on his girlfriend's forehead.

彼得上火車之前，突然回頭在他女朋友的額頭上大聲親了一下。

smack-dab

5 副 恰好地；不偏不倚地

My car bumped **smack-dab** into the police car.

我的車不偏不倚地撞到警車。

smack 就是「海洛因」，**smack out** 就是「吸海洛因吸得很嗨」的意思。

smack off（手淫）源於英國，在英國用得比較多。

smacker 多是爺爺奶奶叫孫子給他們一個大親親（Come here and give me a great big smacker!）。

smart-ass (-arse)

1 名 自以為是、賣弄聰明的人

I enjoy hanging out with Nathan, but he can act like a smart-ass sometimes. I don't even think half of what he says is true.

我很喜歡跟納森一起混，但是他有時很愛賣弄聰明，我甚至覺得他説的話沒一半真的。

2 形 自以為是的

I've had enough of your smart-ass comments. Stop acting like you know everything.

我聽夠你那些自以為是的意見了，不要再一副你什麼都懂的樣子。

smart-mouth

3 動 說話沒大沒小

Kids these days have the habit of smart-mouthing to their parents, but it's really the parents' fault for not teaching them discipline.

這年頭小孩習慣跟爸媽講話沒大沒小，這其實是爸媽的錯，是他們沒管好孩子。

smart 原指「聰明」，smart-ass 和原意有點關聯，指「自以為是的人」，他們對什麼都有意見，在英國 ass 的拼法為 arse，但兩個字都是一樣的意思。

smart-mouth 是美國俚語，是指一個人沒分寸，對人説話不尊重。

204

smashing

[ˈsmæʃɪŋ]

1

形 很棒、很讚

The outfit that Jules wore to the party the other night was simply **smashing**. She received so many compliments.

茱兒那天晚上穿去派對的衣服真好看，大家讚不絕口。

smashed

[smæʃt]

2

形 喝醉的

After the concert, the band got **smashed** with some of their fans backstage.

演唱會結束後，樂團在後台跟一群歌迷一起喝酒喝到醉。

3

形 吸毒吸得很嗨

Most of the people at the rave last night were **smashed**.

昨晚狂歡派對上，好多人都吸毒吸得很嗨。

smashing 最常用來表示「很棒」、「很讚」。如果有人說某個東西很smashing，通常會加強語氣。

smashed 多用於形容「喝醉」，也可以形容「吸毒吸得很嗨」。

smoke [smok]

1 名 香菸

I hate it when strangers try to bum a smoke from me:

我最討厭陌生人跟我討菸抽了。

2 動 殺死

The cowboy smoked the villain in a duel at the end of the movie.

電影結尾，牛仔跟壞人決鬥時，把壞人殺了！

holy smoke

3 嘆 表示驚訝、興奮

Holy smoke! Look at how fast that horse is running.

天啊！你看，那匹馬跑得多快。

　　不管你走到哪，總是有人在 smoke a cigarette（抽菸）或是買 smoke（香菸），好玩的是，原來表示抽菸的動詞 smoke，反而比 cigarette 更常用來表示「香菸」。

　　用 smoke 表示「殺死」的用法源於美國，電影、歌曲裡較常聽到，日常對話中則比較少用。

　　當你覺得很驚訝、受到驚嚇或很興奮的時候，就可以說 Holy smoke! 來表達你的情緒，相同的感嘆用語還有 holy cow、holy Moses、holy moly。

snatch [snætʃ]

1 動 搶劫、盜取

The thieves **snatched** a bunch of jewels from Tiffany's on Fifth Avenue last night.

竊賊昨晚在第五大道的珠寶名店 Tiffany 偷走了一堆珠寶。

2 動 綁架

I read a story the other day where a child was **snatched** from her bedroom while she was sleeping.

我前幾天看到一則故事說，有個小女孩在自己房間睡覺時被綁架。

3 名 女性的外陰

Some women find it offensive when a man calls the pudendum a **snatch**.

有些女生會覺得男生用「鮑魚」來稱呼女生的陰部很不禮貌。

snatch 原意是「抓取」，以上俚語用法就是從原意衍生出來的。snatch 最常用來表示「綁架」，以前報紙都用 snatch 報導小孩被綁架的新聞，之所以會用這個字，是想降低衝擊。「搶劫案」也可稱為 snatch，電影 *Snatch*《偷拐搶騙》就是描述幾個搶匪犯下大宗珠寶搶案。

15 到 30 歲之間的人聽到 snatch，可能不會想到綁架或搶劫，而會想到女性的陰部。這種用法很粗俗，多數女性都不喜歡聽到這個字。

snot rag

1
名 手帕

I never understood why people carry **snot rags** around with them. Tissues are much more sanitary.

我一直不懂為什麼有人想帶手帕，面紙衛生多了。

snot-nosed

2
形 幼稚、自負或可鄙的人

Ivy is a **snot-nosed** brat. She is used to getting everything she wants from her parents.

艾芙這個小屁孩真被寵壞了，她習慣想要什麼就找爸媽要。

snotty   [ˋsnɑtɪ]

3
形 驕傲自滿

Lynn always acts like she's better than us. She's the **snottiest** person I've ever met.

琳恩每次都一副高人一等的樣子，她是我見過最臭屁的人了。

4 形 卑劣的

I never befriend people who are **snotty** to others, since I know they'd be snotty to me one day, too.

我從來不跟對別人不好的人做朋友，因為我知道有天他們也會這樣對我。

5 形 流鼻涕的

Diane wiped his son's **snotty** nose.

黛安幫她兒子擦鼻涕。

snot 指「鼻涕」，上述的俚語中只有幾個和原意直接相關。**snot rag**（手帕），多數人在買手帕時並不會把手帕稱作 snot rag，但一旦用手帕擤過鼻涕，新手帕就變成 snot rag 了。

這裡面 **snot-nosed** 最常用，常被用來形容孩子。多數人都會用 snot-nosed brat，加上 brat 強調出那個人有多「幼稚、自負又討人厭」！

snuff [snʌf]

1
名 古柯鹼

When Joseph was in college, he became addicted to snuff. He eventually checked himself into rehab and is clean now.

約瑟大學時染上了古柯鹼，最後他自己跑去戒毒中心，現在不碰毒品了。

snuff it

2
慣 死亡

My goldfish snuffed it when my roommate put too much food in the fish tank.

我室友倒太多飼料到魚缸了，把我的金魚搞死了。

snuff out

3
片 動 謀殺

The couple hired a hit man to snuff out their next-door neighbor.

那對夫妻雇了殺手幹掉隔壁鄰居。

snuff 原意是「聞、吸」，吸毒者和毒販常把古柯鹼稱為 snuff，警察也可能會這麼說，但是一般人通常不會用 snuff 來指古柯鹼。

無論是 snuff it（死亡）或 snuff out（謀殺），都是某人或生物斷氣了。一般人在日常生活中不會用到 snuff out，通常只有犯罪集團裡的人才會用。

son of a bitch

1 〔慣〕狗東西；狗娘養的；混蛋

Sean is a **son of a bitch**. He fired April right on the spot, even though she signed a one-year contract to teach at the school.

西恩真是王八蛋，就算愛普已經跟學校簽了任教一年的約，他還是當場開除她。

son of a gun

2 〔慣〕傢伙

Cindy that **son of a gun** did it again. She borrowed my hairbrush but forgot to put it back. Now I can't find it.

辛蒂那個傢伙又來了，她把我的梳子借走，忘了放回去，我又找不到了。

son of a bitch（狗娘養的）是英國和美國俚語，非常常用，用來稱呼那些冒犯你的混蛋，通常是罵男生，還可縮寫為 S.O.B. 或 SOB。

son of a gun 則是美國和加拿大俚語，多用來形容小孩和青少年，這是一個很老的詞，年紀大的人常說這個字。這個字比較沒那麼粗。

sore [sor]

1 形 生氣的；火大的

Jane was **sore** at her roommate Erin because she told her something in confidence, and Erin ended up telling one of her friends and it got back to Jane.

珍超氣室友艾琳，因為她告訴她一個祕密，結果艾琳把祕密告訴她們的一個朋友，最後傳回珍的耳朵。

sorehead

2 名 生著悶氣的人；輸不起的人

Don't be such a **sorehead**. I was only joking.

不要生悶氣嘛，我只是開開玩笑。

sore loser

3 名 輸不起的人

After Kevin lost the tennis match, he refused to shake his opponent's hand. He's such a **sore loser**.

凱文網球比賽輸了以後，他不肯跟對手握手，真是輸不起的傢伙。

　　sore 原意是「疼痛的」或「令人傷心」，以上三個俚語都互相關聯。sore loser 可描述小孩，也可形容成年人，有時小孩比賽到一半，還沒輸，就不想比了。

　　成年人也常常輸不起，常發生在體育比賽中，有時是選手不服氣，跟對手打架，有時是球迷不服氣，跟對方的球迷打架。

sort [sɔrt]

1 名 漂亮美眉

Check out that **sort** that just sat down. I wonder if she came here alone or with someone.

看看那邊剛坐下的美眉，我想知道她是一個人來的，還是跟別人一起來的。

sort out

2 片 動 解決、處理（問題或困難）

After Matthew moved out of the apartment, he had to come back one more time to get the rest of his things. It was kind of difficult to get things **sorted out** when his ex-girlfriend was home.

麥修搬家後還得回舊家一趟拿剩下的東西，不過他前女友在家，要把東西處理好有點困難。

sort someone out

3 片 動 痛毆

When Dave was at the bar, some asshole pinched his girlfriend's bum. When he didn't apologize, Dave decided to **sort him out**.

那天大衛在酒吧時，一個混蛋捏了他女友的屁股，那人不道歉，大衛決定痛扁他一頓。

it takes all sorts

4 📖 世界之大，無奇不有；一樣米養百樣人

Grace eats soup with a straw. Well, **it takes all sorts** (to make a world).

葛蕾絲用吸管喝湯。好吧！這世上什麼人都有。

　　北美的人說 **sort out** 時，指的就是把衣物分成深色和淺色兩堆。上述俚語都源自英國，當然你也會在其他地方聽到，但還是英國最常用。其中最常用的是 sort out，「解決」、「處理」的意思。其次常用的是 **sort**，指「漂亮迷人的女生」，男人比較常用。

　　當你聽到 **It takes all sorts** (to make a world). ，代表說話者認為某人的行為很奇怪，但這世上什麼人都有，只好接納或容忍對方。

spaced

1 形 吸毒後恍惚的狀態

Paul was totally **spaced** on weed when I saw him last night. It was impossible to have a rational conversation with him.

昨晚我看保羅吸大麻吸得茫茫的,我根本不能跟他正常談話。

space cake

2 名 大麻做的蛋糕

When you go to Amsterdam, you'll have to try a **space cake**. It is on the menu in many coffee houses there.

如果你去阿姆斯特丹,一定要嚐嚐大麻蛋糕,那裡很多咖啡店都有這道。

space out

3 片 動 暫時脫離現實,做白日夢

After a boring day at work, Grace likes to go home, put her headphones on, and **space out** to classical music.

一天無聊的工作結束,葛雷絲喜歡回家、戴上耳機、悠遊在古典音樂的世界,什麼都不管。

spacey/spacy ['spesɪ]

4 形 混亂瘋狂，與現實脫節的

Leslie has been acting a bit spacey lately. Is she on some kind of medication?

萊絲莉最近瘋瘋的，她是不是在吃什麼藥？

　　space cake 是阿姆斯特丹（Amsterdam）的特色餐點，當地人把大麻或是有迷幻作用的菇類做成蛋糕或巧克力布朗尼。一旦吃進了這些毒品，過陣子你就會覺得 spaced（飄飄欲仙）。

　　你也可能會變得 spacey/spacy（混亂瘋狂），與現實脫節，不過，感覺 spacey 倒不一定要吸毒才會發生。

　　每個人隨時都可以脫離現實，做白日夢，這時你可以說你 space out 了。

spew [spju]

1 動 嘔吐

The rollercoaster ride was too much for Ben. He **spewed** up as soon as he got off.

班受不了雲霄飛車，他一下來就吐了。

2 動 坦承

Amber, if you don't **spew** everything about your date, I will scream!

安柏，如果你不把約會的細節交代清楚，我要尖叫了！

spew chunks

3 片 動 嘔吐

Vincent got food poisoning from eating seafood at the restaurant and **spewed chunks** later that night.

文森吃了那餐廳的海鮮，結果食物中毒，當晚狂吐。

spew 和 spew chunks 最常用來指「嘔吐」，如果有人 spew，是指突然爆發、吐得滿身。

記住嘔吐時那種食物往上衝的感覺後，你就可以理解 spew 和「坦承」、「招認」的關聯了。

214

spill [spɪl]

1 名 金額很少的小費

The waitress was horrible so my friend gave her a **spill**.

那個女服務生很粗魯，所以我朋友只給她一點點小費。

2 動 坦承

OK, **spill** it. I want to hear all about your vacation and the good looking Australian man you met!

快給我通通招來，你的假期還有你遇到的那個澳洲帥哥，我都想知道！

3 動 洩漏祕密

For Christmas, Dad was going to give Mom two tickets for a cruise. Brendan's little brother was the only one that knew about it, and he accidentally **spilled** the surprise.

聖誕節禮物爸爸想送媽媽兩張郵輪票，只有布蘭登的小弟知道，結果他不小心說溜嘴。

spill the beans

4 慣 不小心洩漏祕密

Little kids are not good at keeping secrets. They always **spill the beans**.

小孩子不會保守祕密，每次都說溜嘴。

spill one's guts

圓 揭露、全部說出來

Isabelle wrote a long letter to Tom, in which she spilled her guts about her feelings for him.

伊莎貝爾寫了一封長信給湯姆，向他傾訴所有心意。

spill 原意「潑出來」、「濺出來」，這幾個俚語都表示「無法保守祕密」，要記住 spill one's guts 是「全招」的意思，spill the beans 則是表「不小心說出口」，意思不太一樣。

split [splɪt]

1 📖 洩漏祕密；背叛、出賣

Allison, my so-called best friend whom I told my secrets to, after 10 years of friendship just up and **splits** on me one day.

我什麼祕密都跟我所謂的好朋友艾利森說，就在我們的認識十年後的某一天，她竟然出賣我。

2 📖 離開

Sorry, but I have to **split** if I'm going to make this train!

不好意思，如果我想趕上這班火車，我得閃了！

3 📖 分享

I would love to have dessert, but I can't eat the whole thing. Want to **split** a chocolate torte with me?

我想吃甜點，但是我吃不完一份，想不想跟我分一塊巧克力蛋糕？

　　split 表示「分開、裂開、爆開或撕裂」，這和表示「分享」的俚語用法也有些關聯。每次有什麼東西太大份吃不完或用不完時，split（分享）通常就是最好的處理方式。

　　朋友之間也常用 split 來表示「離開」。如果你 split 或是 have to split，你無須鄭重道別，你可以隨時起身離開。

spook [spuk]

1 名 驚嚇

That movie sure gave a lot of people a **spook**. Some people even screamed out in the theater.

那部電影真的嚇到了很多人，有人還在電影院裡尖叫呢！

2 動 受驚嚇

After hearing about the old dead woman and how she still walks the marshes, I was **spooked** and couldn't fall asleep last night.

聽了那個往生的老婆婆在沼澤間流連的故事後，我真的嚇壞了，昨晚睡不著。

3 名 黑人

Even though it's a racist slur, **spook** is still used sometimes in the United States to refer to black people.

雖然黑鬼是個充滿種族歧視意味的稱號，在美國有時還是被用來稱呼黑人。

4 名 臥底或間諜

The **spook** knew he was about to blow his cover, but he couldn't do a thing about it.

臥底知道自己的身分就要被揭穿，卻一點辦法也沒有。

　　spook 最常用來表示「受到驚嚇的」，自有鬼魂、妖精這些概念存在以來，這個字就出現了。有時候人們就會用 spook 表示「鬼」。

　　用 spook 稱呼黑人，是極度冒犯詆毀人的說法，帶有歧視之意。

spunk [spʌŋk]

1

名 精神、勇氣

I spoke to a veteran of World War II, and he said that half the men in his platoon wouldn't have made it through the war if it wasn't for their **spunk**.

我曾跟一個二戰的退伍軍人聊天，他說要不是靠著意志力，他那一排有一半的人撐不了那麼久。

2

名 精液

Jerking off in bed, he got some **spunk** on his sheets.

他在床上打手槍，精液沾到床單上了。

spunky

3

形 生氣勃勃的

Mrs. Brown is the **spunkiest** 102-year-old woman I've ever had the pleasure of knowing.

布朗太太是我有幸認識最有活力的 102 歲老太太了。

spunk 或 **spunky** 最好的解釋就是，看起來心胸開闊、面帶微笑、活著就覺得很快樂的人。

老人家用這個字描述他們的孫子孫女，或是描述他們以前多有朝氣、多有精力。年輕人用這個字，則多是描述長者生氣勃勃。

stiff [stɪf]

1 形 喝醉的

Meg and Rea were **stiff** from having drunk wine all afternoon.

梅格和瑞雅喝了一下午酒，都喝掛了。

2 名 醉漢、酒鬼

Don't pour that **stiff** another drink. He already smells like he has whiskey running through his veins.

別再灌那個酒鬼了，他已經聞起來好像血管裡都是威士忌了。

3 名 屍體

Working in a morgue, you see a lot of **stiffs**.

在停屍間裡工作會看到很多屍體。

4 形 非常貴的

I couldn't believe how **stiff** the price was on those earrings.

我真不敢相信那對耳環的價錢會這麼貴。

5 **名** 死板、無聊的人

I never liked dating Justin. He was such a **stiff** and kissing him was like kissing a dead fish.

我一直不喜歡跟賈斯汀約會，他這個人超無聊的，親他就跟親死魚一樣。

6 **動** 欺騙、詐騙

Sometimes Ryan would walk out of Denny's and **stiff** the waitress.

有時候雷恩會走出丹尼斯餐廳，騙騙女服務生。

stiff 最典型的用法就是用來形容「很濃烈或很有效的」飲料或藥。

醫學界和警界則用 stiff 表示「屍體」，這種說法對死者很不敬，因此不會在家屬面前說這個字。

stiff 還常常用來表示「昂貴的」，去買東西沒看標價、之後被價錢嚇一大跳的人，都會說這個字。

stone-broke

1

形 身無分文

Even if Pam wanted to leave, she is **stone-broke** and can't afford a plane ticket.

帕瑪很想離開，但是她實在破產了，連機票也買不起。

stoned

2

形 吸了毒或喝醉酒

After getting **stoned** with the boys in the living room, she went to the kitchen to get something to eat.

跟男生在客廳裡喝茫了以後，她走到廚房找東西吃。

stone-faced

3

形 面無表情

Betty sat **stone-faced** as her daughter told her the bad news.

貝蒂的女兒跟她說壞消息的時候，她面無表情地坐著。

　　stone（石頭）死死的，不會動，這樣想比較容易記住俚語用法。

　　stone-broke 指一個人「窮到極點」，想弄錢也弄不到。

　　stoned 指吸毒或喝酒後，人目光呆滯、恍恍惚惚的樣子。

　　stone-faced，就跟塊石頭一樣，坐在那裡，表情沒有任何變化，這個字源自英國，英國人就是出了名的不太顯露內心的情緒，有點冷酷、難以接近。

straight [stret]

1

形 異性戀者

Nowadays, you can't tell who is **straight** and who isn't.

現在你根本看不出誰是異性戀，誰是同性戀。

2

形 沒有摻雜其他東西的；未稀釋的

I will have a **straight** scotch, please.

請給我一杯純的威士忌。

3

形 態度、習俗或外表保守傳統

Some people think Mary is too **straight** for her own good. She needs to expand her horizons on so many different levels of her life.

有些人覺得瑪莉太保守了，她應該多方面擴展生活視野才對。

4

形 誠實可靠的

You have to be **straight** with me. Do you think my portfolio is worth showing to any galleries?

你老實告訴我，你覺得我的作品值得拿去畫廊展示嗎？

straight up

5

慣 真的；的確

I'll tell you **straight up** that if your grades don't improve, you're going to fail this course.

我就跟你直說了，如果你的成績再不進步，你這科會被當。

straight-edge

6 形 不吸毒、不抽菸、不喝酒

Those who have chosen a **straight-edge** lifestyle, more power to you. However, it isn't something I want for myself, at least not for now.

對那些不喝酒、不抽菸、不吸毒的人,在此致上我的敬意,不過我不想過這種生活,至少現在不想。

straight 原意「直的」,它的俚語用法都有「自然、不摻雜、不複雜」的精神,如不摻水的酒、保守的態度,或者是為人誠實可靠,到不使用任何對健康有害的化學物品。

straight-edge,中譯為「直刃族」,始於美國八〇年代,當時美國人常把龐克搖滾樂和吸毒聯想在一起,後來樂團 Minor Threat 的主唱發起一個 straight-edge 運動,主張不吸毒、不抽大麻、不喝酒、不濫交,不穿戴皮草,推行回歸簡單生活、降低慾望,其他樂團也跟進,以音樂推廣理念,到九〇年代中期,更散播到歐洲和其他地區。

straight-edge 被縮寫為 sXe,認同這個理念的人,會在身上或衣服上畫 X 或刺 sXe 表明自己的立場。

strung out   [strʌŋ]

1 ⊞ 情緒低落、心情很亂

Delilah is totally **strung out** from taking care of her elderly parents, her kids, and working full time. She seriously needs a holiday.

蒂萊拉要照顧年長的雙親和小孩，又有全職工作，真的累壞了，很需要放假。

2 ⊞ 吸毒、酗後很疲累的狀態

When Dominic came in to work on Monday, you could tell he was still **strung out** from the weekend bender.

多明尼克星期一來上班時，可以看出他週末狂歡後還沒恢復精神。

3 ⊞ 毒癮發作很痛苦的

Being **strung out** when you're trying to quit heroin is more horrible than a bad day on it.

要戒海洛因的時候，毒癮發作比打太多還難受。

string 是指用繩子掛起來，要了解 strung out 的意思，可想像一個人被夾在曬衣繩上的模樣，不過可不是享受日光浴，而是在刮風下雨中冷得發抖，描繪出人在 strung out 時生心理的感受。

strung out 最常用來形容「毒癮發作感到痛苦」，戒毒是個很痛苦的過程，曾經戒過像是 snuff（古柯鹼）、smack（海洛因）這類毒品的人，都經歷過 strung out 所帶來的痛苦。

suck [sʌk]

1 動 爛透了

You **suck**! It's not fair that I have to work a full day and you can go home at noon.

你真是太爛了！我要工作一整天，你卻中午就可以回家，太不公平了。

"My mom won't let me go to the party this Saturday. She says I have to stay home and study."

"That **sucks**. There'll be other parties in the future, though."

「我媽不讓我參加週六的派對，她說我要待在家念書。」

「爛死了！不過以後還有很多派對啦！」

sucky

2 形 討人厭的、不愉快的

Ted is in such a **sucky** mood tonight. It happens every time he has a bad day at work.

泰德今天晚上心情超差，每次他白天工作不順就會這樣。

suck 原指「吸吮」，當俚語時 suck 最常用來表達個人對某個人或某件事的反應，表示你生氣、不滿意、很失望、無法接受，常以開玩笑、不生氣的口吻表達，我們能夠從當事人的語氣聽出其中的差別。朋友之間通常會以 You suck. 或 That sucks. 來使用 suck 這個字。

sucky（不愉快的）也源於美國，相當常用。

sucker [ˈsʌkɚ]

1 名 棒棒糖

Lili bought two **suckers** at the candy store.

莉莉在糖果店買了兩根棒棒糖。

2 名 容易受騙的人

You are such a **sucker**! You believe everything!

你耳根子太軟了！什麼你都信！

3 名 因被笑而改變主意的人

I wasn't going to go to the movies but I am such a **sucker** for chick-flick tear-jerkers that I had to say yes.

我本來不想去看催淚愛情片的，但別人一慫恿我，我就答應了。

suck up to

4 片 動 諂媚

Laura is shamelessly **sucking up to** her boss because she wants to get that promotion.

蘿拉不要臉地拍老闆馬屁，因為她想升職。

sucker-punch

5 動 出其不意地攻擊

During the World Cup, one of the fans sucker-punched the guy next to him because he was cheering for the other team.

世界盃期間，一個球迷出其不意地攻擊旁邊的觀眾，因為他幫另一隊加油。

suck face

6 慣 熱吻

Rob and Jackie are in the back room sucking face.

羅柏和潔姬在後面的房間喇舌。

　　sucker 表示「棒棒糖」只用於美國，其他英語國家多用 lolli（lollipop 的簡稱）。

　　sucker（被激而改變主意的人；容易受騙的人）和 suck up to（諂媚）都有負面意義。

　　sucker-punch 源於美國，是出其不意地攻擊人，這種方式通常會讓被打的人很生氣。

　　suck face 源自美國，如果你想像 suck face 的動作，一定會覺得很好玩，suck face 是熱情的吻法。

surf [sɝf]

1 動 漫遊網路

I don't understand how some people can spend hours **surfing** the Web.

我真不懂為什麼有人花好幾個小時掛在網路上。

surf bum

2 名 常去衝浪的衝浪客

Along the coast in California you will see hundreds of **surf bums**. They will travel up and down the coast, depending on where the best waves are.

沿著加州海岸你會看到許多衝浪客，哪裡有最好的浪，他們就會沿著岸南北跑。

surfie

3 名 衝浪迷

Australia and New Zealand are the breeding grounds for **surfies**.

澳洲和紐西蘭是衝浪迷的發源地。

surfboard

4 名 平胸的女生；太平公主

Dan is into **surfboards**. He doesn't find large-chested women attractive.

丹喜歡太平公主，不覺得胸大的女生有吸引力。

channel surf

5 慣 用遙控器快速瀏覽頻道

Andy likes to **channel surf** while the commercials are on.

安迪喜歡在廣告時間不斷地轉台。

surf 當俚語是指「上網」，現在網路很發達，常有人閒閒沒事、掛網聊天、四處瀏覽。

surf bum 和 **surfie** 都指「衝浪迷」，surfie 是澳洲、紐西蘭的俚語。

有些人看電視喜歡一直轉台，這個動作就叫 **channel surf** 或 channel hop。

sweet [swit]

1

嘆 表同意

Sweet. I couldn't have thought of a better gift idea for Joan myself. She will love it.

太好了！我自己想不到更好的禮物可以送給瓊安，她一定會很喜歡的。

2

形 令人滿意的；可以接受的

After rearranging the flowers the way she wanted them, she thought the bouquet looked sweet.

她用自己想要的方式重新調整過花後，覺得那束花看起來漂亮多了。

sweet pea

3

名 寶貝（表鍾愛的稱呼）

Jill's grandfather has been calling her sweet pea ever since the day she was born. She can't remember if he has ever called her by her real name.

吉兒從出生爺爺就一直叫她「寶貝」，她實在不記得他哪一次叫過她的名字。

sweetie

4 图 親愛的（表愛意的稱呼）

The waitress at the diner that I go to every morning for coffee calls me sweetie. We've known each other for years.

我每天早上買咖啡那間餐廳女服務生都叫我親愛的，我們認識好幾年了。

sweet talk

5 慣 用甜言蜜語勸誘

Everyone knows that if you want something from Dan, all you have to do is sweet talk him. He is such a sucker.

每個人都知道想從丹身上得到什麼，跟他說點甜言蜜語就好了，他耳根子很軟。

　　上面這幾個字都具有正面意味，大家常用 sweet 表示「極好的」、「讚透的」。sweet 還未完全取代 awesome（讚透了）這個字，但是使用率一樣頻繁，甚至更多。

　　sweetie 和 sweet pea 都是表示愛意的稱呼，夫妻、情侶、對小孩說話的大人或女性朋友之間打招呼時常用這些字。

　　sweet pea 多是老一輩的人跟小孩子說話時會用到，你也可能會聽到老先生用 sweet pea 稱呼自己的老伴。

switch on

1

片動 （吸毒）上癮

Many people who **switch on** to drugs at a young age do it as a result of peer pressure.

很多人年紀輕輕就染毒，是出於同儕壓力。

2

片動 變得興奮

Eva didn't want to go out tonight but she **switched on** once she took a shower and turned on her favorite "get ready" music.

伊娃今晚本來不想出門的，但是她洗完澡，打開她最愛的「準備好」音樂後，興致就來了。

3

片動 讓人性興奮

Even the tiniest smile, caress, or kiss from her lover would **switch** her **on** in ways that no other guy has done before.

即使只是情人輕輕一笑、愛撫或親吻，都會讓她興奮不已，其他男人也沒給她這種感覺。

4

片動 反應快、機靈

After her first cup of morning coffee, Nina would be **switched on** for the rest of the day. Before her coffee she would still be half asleep.

妮娜早上喝完她第一杯咖啡之後，接下來一整天都精力十足、反應明快，沒喝咖啡前她還半睡半醒的。

switcheroo [ˌswɪtʃəˈru]

5 名 意外的變化

"Let's do the old **switcheroo** in the bottom of the ninth and win this game," said the coach of the Bobcats.

山貓隊的教練說：「九局下半我們來個大逆轉，贏得這場比賽吧！」

　　switch on 的原意是「開」，上述俚語用法和原意很接近。對毒品 switch on 可不是一件好事；表示過去從不吸毒的人突然「對毒品上癮」了。對毒品 switch on 的人，會一直需要毒品，就像開關一直開著，沒辦法關掉一樣。

　　「被挑起性慾」、「反應變得明快」或「情緒興奮」這些過程都像是有人打開了你的開關一樣，而這些感覺也都來得快、去得快，這幾個俚語都相當常用。

　　switcheroo 比較少用，表示「意外的轉變、逆轉」，像電影結局大逆轉，就可以用 switcheroo 來形容。

123

tackiness [ˋtækɪnɪs]

1 名 粗俗無禮

Tackiness is something that I do not tolerate in a man. Whoever I date has to look neat and clean.

我絕對沒法忍受男人沒教養，跟我約會的人一定要整齊、乾淨。

tacky [ˋtækɪ]

2 形 品味很差的；低俗的

Cindy looks so **tacky** in that short nylon skirt and those plastic high heels. It's OK if she wants to look sexy, but there are more elegant ways to go about it.

辛蒂穿那條尼龍短裙和塑膠高跟鞋，看起沒品味。她想性感一點沒關係，但還有更多高尚的穿法。

這兩個字之中 tacky 最常用，它表示「沒有品味、低俗」。我們到國外旅行，可能會發現在自己國家被視為沒品味的穿著，在國外可能很流行，有很大的文化差異。

take a chill pill

1 價 放鬆

Honestly, **take a chill pill**! You've been running around the house like a chicken with its head cut off.

說真的,放輕鬆點嘛!你就像隻無頭蒼蠅一樣,在家裡跑來跑去。

take five

2 價 工作中短暫的休息

OK, people, we have two more scenes to shoot, but in the mean time **take five**. The lighting needs to be changed.

好了,各位,我們還有兩場戲要拍,不過現在先休息一下,要換一下燈光。

take it easy

3 價 帶有鼓勵意味的道別語

As Matthew walked away, he turned around and said, "**Take it easy**. See you next time."

馬修要走的時候,轉過身來說:「放輕鬆吧,下次見。」

　　為什麼要說 **take a chill pill** 呢? 因為人無法自己放鬆冷靜的時候,可以去找醫生開些鎮靜劑(chill pill),chill 俚語意「放鬆」。

　　take five 表示一個人需要停下來深呼吸一下,數到五,再繼續工作。**take it easy** 的意思是「放輕鬆」,請對方好好保重,用這句話道別,通常很快會再見面。

take a rain check

1 慣 延期或改期

I'd love to go out with you guys tonight, but I'm going to have to **take a rain check**. I have a meeting first thing tomorrow and I have to get my notes in order.

我今晚真的很想跟你們出去，但我要跟你們改約了，明天一早有個會要開，我得把筆記整理好。

take the piss out of

2 慣 戲謔、嘲笑

I loved hanging out with my English friends because they're always **taking the piss out of** someone. It's always a night full of laughs.

我很喜歡跟我那些英國朋友混在一起，因為他們一直取笑人，大伙一整晚笑個不停。

　　rain check 本來是球賽遇雨停賽，主辦單位會發一張 rain check 讓你在期限內免費再看一次比賽，後來延伸到其他地方，像是在商店拿到 rain check，表示你想要的東西現在缺貨，你可以改天再來買或換。另外，當你想跟人改約時間，就可以説 take a rain check。

　　take the piss out of 源於英國，表示「嘲笑、取笑」某人或某事，在英國相當普遍，但是北美地區並不這麼用。

take down

1 片動 殺死

Dan is a trained marine who knows how to **take down** a man in numerous ways, including with his bare hands.

丹是訓練有素的海軍陸戰隊隊員，知道好幾種殺人的方法，包括徒手殺人。

take out

2 片動 殺死、毀滅

The general told his men to **take out** anything and everything in their path.

將軍命令下屬消滅路上遇到的一切。

take names

3 慣 記下壞學生的名字

Elizabeth was having trouble with the class. She needed to **take names** before continuing on with the lesson.

伊麗莎白上課的時候遇到麻煩，她得記下學生的名字，再繼續上課。

　　take down 和 **take out** 可以互換使用，算相當普遍，很少用來描述個人殺人或毀滅行為，它們通常是用來描述電影或書中所發生的事件，take down 和 take out 表示「殺人」是相當殘忍無情的說法。

tick off

1 片動 斥責

In order to show the children that you mean business, you have to **tick** them **off** whenever they are out of line.

為了讓孩子們知道你是認真的，他們不守規矩的時候，你得電電他們。

ticked off

2 形 生氣、惱怒

I was so **ticked off** this morning. The bus was late, I wasn't able to grab my morning coffee, and at the last minute, the boss called a mandatory meeting.

我今天早上超火大的，公車來晚了，沒時間買咖啡，老闆又突然下令要開會。

兩個用法中最常用的是「生氣」，屬於比較委婉的說法，說明某人很「火大」。比 **ticked off** 更強烈的說法是 pissed off，在公開場合或是跟小孩說話的時候，最好用 ticked off，這樣不會冒犯別人，也不必在小孩面前罵髒話。

ticker [ˈtɪkɚ]

1 名 手錶

My grandmother always calls her watch a **ticker**. I think this sounds kind of funny.

我奶奶老把她的手錶叫作滴答,我覺得聽起來很有趣。

2 名 心臟

"Well, looks like you are in great health; your **ticker** has at least another 20 years ahead of it," said the doctor.

醫生說:「嗯,看起來你的健康狀況很好,你的心臟還可以繼續跳個 20 年。」

手錶秒針走的時候,會發出滴滴答答的聲音,英文的擬聲詞是 tick,因此用 **ticker** 指「手錶」。

因為心臟和手錶一樣,每隔一段時間就會動一下,ticker 也被用來指「心臟」。

tickle the ivories

1 慣 彈鋼琴

Ivan was invited to **tickle the ivories** to liven things up at the party.

艾文受邀到派對來彈琴助興。

tickle one's pickle

2 慣 自慰

I don't understand why men are always **tickling their pickles**. Read a book or something!

我真不懂男人怎麼老是打手槍,看看書,做點別的吧!

tickle one's fancy

3 慣 享受自己喜歡做的事

"What do you want to do tonight?"

"Whatever **tickles your fancy**. I'm easy."

「你今晚想做什麼?」

「你想做什麼就做吧,我都可以。」

tickle 原意是「搔癢」,讓你覺得癢和興奮,俚語和原意有些關聯。不管是鋼琴琴鍵或男性生殖器,都和觸摸有關。

tickled pink

1 慣 非常高興

My mother was **tickled pink** that I would be home for the holidays.

我假日的時候會在家，我媽高興得要死。

slap and tickle

2 名 調情；打情罵俏

The couple engaged in a bit of **slap and tickle** on the grass.

那對情侶在草地上打情罵俏。

　　tickle 原意是「搔癢」，讓你覺得癢和興奮，俚語和原意有些關聯。**tickled pink** 最常用，指「非常高興」，想像人高興時臉紅的樣子，就很容易記住這個意思了。

　　slap and tickle 是英國俚語，意思是情侶間的打情罵俏，親親抱抱的樣子。

tight [taɪt]

1

形 因缺錢而生活困難的

Times are **tight** right now. He has to save every penny he makes.

現在生活很艱難,他賺的每分錢都得存下來。

tight-ass

2

名 自私、小氣、吝嗇的人

She is such a **tight-ass**. She never puts any money into the office pot for birthday parties for the coworkers.

她是隻鐵公雞,從來不會把錢投進辦公室裡為同事慶生的募款箱。

3

名 過度壓抑、保守的人

Jim's a real **tight-ass**. He should let loose and have some fun once in a while.

吉姆真的太壓抑了,他該放鬆一下,偶爾找點樂子。

tight-assed

4

形 吝嗇的、小氣的

Sometimes it is good to be **tight-assed**. It's frustrating to watch people throw their money around.

有時候還是節儉一點比較好,看人隨便亂花錢,還真令人洩氣。

tightwad

[ˈtaɪtˌwɑd]

5 名 吝嗇鬼

Mike is such a **tightwad**. He keeps a record of every penny he spends and never buys anything for anyone.

麥可是個守財奴，花的每分錢都要記帳，而且從來不會買東西送人。

以上五個詞義都很相近，常常可以互換使用，如果有人想要存錢，或是沒有太多錢可以花，他會把錢緊緊帶在身邊，只在需要的時候拿出來，因此我們會用 **tight** 描述「節儉」、「吝嗇」或因缺錢而生活困難的人。

tight [taɪt]

1 形 喝醉的

After a few drinks with her coworkers, she felt a little **tight**.

跟同事喝了幾杯之後，她覺得有點醉了。

2 形 友好的、親密的

It's amazing how **tight** we've become after we broke up. Our relationship is better now than it was when we were dating.

真不可思議，分手後我們反而變得更親密，現在的關係比交往的時候還要好。

tightlipped

3 形 守口如瓶

The CEO remained **tightlipped** about his company's rumored merger.

總裁對公司合併的傳聞守口如瓶。

如果你跟某個人無話不談，他們願意為你做任何事，你也願意為他們做任何事，那你和這個人就很tight（親密），用法源於美國，高中生和大學生經常說這個字。

真的跟你很tight的人，也會是個tightlipped（守口如瓶）的人，把嘴唇（lips）閉緊（tight），表示你不會讓祕密從你的雙唇之間洩漏出去。

toss [tɔs]

1 動 搜索房宅

The policeman had a search warrant so they could **toss** the place.

警察有搜索令，所以他們可以搜查這個地方。

2 動 擊敗

The Baboons **tossed** the visiting team in this Saturday's game.

這星期六的比賽狒狒隊擊敗了客隊。

3 名 沒有價值、用處的人

Why did Dora marry that **toss**? He's such a mooch.

朵拉幹嘛嫁給那個廢人，他是個寄生蟲。

tosser

4 名 白痴、笨蛋、沒用的人

Katie's boyfriend can be a **tosser** sometimes, but she still loves him.

凱蒂的男友有時很白痴，但她還是愛他。

toss (one's) cookies

5 慣 嘔吐

While on vacation, Andrew **tossed cookies** for two days from food poisoning.

安德魯度假時食物中毒，整整吐了兩天。

toss 通常是指「搜查」，像是要找犯罪證據或分贓，會破壞現場。

toss 表示「擊敗」，用於澳洲，其他地方較少聽到這個意思。

toss 或 **tosser** 表示「廢人」或「笨蛋」，用於英國、南非。

toss (one's) cookies 源於美國，生動地描繪「嘔吐」的畫面，當然吐出來的不一定是餅乾。

tough break

1 名 倒楣、不幸

Losing that scholarship was a **tough break** for Jeff. After the car accident, he was no longer able to play for the baseball team and lost his free ride to college.

失去那筆獎學金對傑夫來説真是太慘了，車禍以後他就不能再打棒球，也沒辦法免費讀大學了。

tough luck

2 嘆 不行

"Mom, I want to stay up and watch the show."

"**Tough luck**. It's past your bedtime, and you have to get up for school in the morning!"

「媽，我想晚點睡，看這個節目。」

「不行！現在已經過了你的上床時間，而且你明天一早還要上學呢！」

要是有人運氣不好，這幾個有趣的字就可以派上用場了，**tough luck** 表示 that's too bad（太慘了），通常諷刺、嘲笑的口吻，多是父母對小孩或老師對學生説的，用意是告訴孩子或學生你不管他們有什麼理由，因為你已經決定了！

tough shit

1 嘆 不幸

"I really want to go to Brad's party."

"Well, **tough shit**. You pissed him off too many times, so he didn't want to invite you."

「我真的很想參加布來德的派對。」

「太不幸了,誰叫你惹火他這麼多次,他不想邀你。」

tough titty

2 嘆 倒楣、厄運

"I lost my week's pay at the blackjack table."

"**Tough titty**. Who told you to gamble in the first place?"

「我玩 21 點,把這星期的薪水輸光了。」

「真倒楣!誰叫你先拿去賭呢?」

要是有人運氣不好,這幾個有趣的字就可以派上用場了,通常是諷刺、嘲笑的口氣。

tough shit 最常用,意思是「真倒楣、好衰」。

tough titty 是英國俚語,美國人很少説,老一輩的人最常説這個字。

tough guy

1 名 意志堅定、不易屈服的人

Don't pretend you're such a **tough guy**. I saw you get teary-eyed in the movie theater.

別裝出一副硬漢的樣子,我看到你在電影院裡眼眶都濕了。

tough cookie

2 名 個性堅強的人

Ray is one **tough cookie**. He fell down on the playground and broke his arm, but he hardly shed a tear.

雷真是個性堅強的小孩,他在遊樂場裡跌倒摔斷了手,但是一滴眼淚也沒掉。

tough nut

3 名 頑固的人

Quintin is a **tough nut**. I try to make working with him pleasant, but he doesn't make things easy for anyone in the office.

昆汀真難搞,我想讓大家跟他共事愉快,但他還是讓辦公室裡的人感到頭痛。

tough love

4 名 嚴厲的愛；強制手段

Winnie maxed out her credit card on designer clothes. Her parents decided to practice **tough love**, so they refused to support her financially.

維妮買設計服飾刷爆卡，為了她好，爸媽決定狠下心不再給她錢。

    tough 原意是「堅韌」、「強勁」，這些俚語都在描述人，體格上的強壯、個性上的堅強，或是思想上的頑固，其中最常用的就是 **tough guy**（硬漢），大多時候用來取笑那些裝出一副沒有感情、不在乎他人感覺的人。

    如果有人想要鼓勵小孩子堅強點，不要被打倒，他們就會對小孩子說，當個 **tough cookie**（勇敢一點），也可以跟那些表現超齡的孩子說：

Stop being such a tough cookie. It is OK to be scared of the dark.
別裝小大人，怕黑又沒關係。

tough love 指的是為讓某人解決自身問題採取的強制手段，像是教練給選手嚴格的訓練，或是父母為了孩子的益處，嚴厲地管教孩子，通常這麼做都是出於善意，且情非得已。

the ax

1 名 開除、炒魷魚

Lars got **the ax** because he took too many cigarette breaks and didn't put enough effort into his work.

萊斯被炒了，因為上班時間太常跑去抽菸休息，工作又不太認真。

the shove

2 名 開除、炒魷魚

Sometimes, it is better to get **the shove** because then you can collect unemployment until another job comes along.

有時候被開除還比較好，因為這樣可以領失業給付，一直領到找到新工作為止。

the boot

3 名 開除、炒魷魚

After working at his new job for only two weeks, Bill was given **the boot**. It was the shortest time he had ever held a job.

比爾的新工作才做了兩星期就被炒了，這是他這輩子工作最短的一次。

the order of the boot

4 慣 打發、拒絕

There was a talent search for the newest up and coming band, and three hundred bands showed up for the audition. All the bands except ten got **the order of the boot**.

他們在找有潛力的新樂團,三百個樂團來參加甄選,最後只剩下十個,其他的都被淘汰了。

　　在美國經常使用 **the ax**,要理解 get the ax(被開除)的意義,不妨想像老闆走進辦公室,在你面前丟一把斧頭(ax),此時要不你走人,要不就是老闆故意要你知難而退!

　　the shove(開除)的概念也很類似,只是不是被踢出公司,而是被推(shove)出去的!

　　the order of the boot 和 **the boot**(開除)都源自英國,美國人會說 the boot,至於 the order of the boot 只有英國人用,這是因為這就好像是對方用靴子(boot)把你踢出某個地方,特別是你工作的地方!

the boondocks [ˈbunˌdɑks]

1 名 荒郊野外；偏僻的鄉下

My cousin and her husband live out in **the boondocks**. They have horses, dogs, and there's one general store 20 minutes from their house.

我表妹和先生住在偏僻的鄉下，有養馬和狗，唯一的雜貨店要 20 分路程。

the burbs [bɚbz]

2 名 市郊（suburb 的縮寫）

People often move out of the city and into **the burbs** after they have kids. It is a better environment to raise children in.

有小孩後，人往往會從市區搬到郊區，那裡環境比較適合孩子成長。

the sticks [stɪks]

3 名 鳥不生蛋，狗不拉屎的地方

Julie lives out in **the sticks**, where shops and services are scarce.

茱莉住在鳥不生蛋，狗不拉屎的地方，幾乎沒有什麼商店和服務。

這幾個詞源自北美洲，使用相當頻繁，有時帶有貶義，用來取笑住在離市區很遠的人，住在這些地方的人也會用這些字開自己的玩笑。

the greatest

1 名 非常優秀的人

Rae's boyfriend Ben is **the greatest**. She is so lucky to have found a man like that!

瑞雅的男友阿班真的很優，找到像他這種男人真幸運！

the pits

2 名 糟糕到極點的人事物

Dana was in bed with a stomachache and all her friends were at the beach for the weekend. Being sick is **the pits**.

黛娜胃痛躺在床上，而她所有朋友都去海邊度週末了，生病遭透了。

the worst

3 名 可鄙、討厭、低下、極糟的事物

Living at home with your parents while you're in college is **the worst**!

上了大學還跟爸媽一起住，真糟！

各行各業、男女老少都使用這幾個詞，這幾個詞其實一看就能了解其意義。pit是地上的窟窿或坑洞。

the heat

[hit]

1 名 **警察**

Late at night, one is guaranteed to see **the heat** pulling people over for routine traffic checks.

夜深時，你一定會看到警察在路邊攔車，執行例行交通檢查。

the joint

[dʒɔɪnt]

2 名 **監獄**

After being in **the joint** for 20 years, he had trouble living in society after he was released.

他在牢裡蹲了 20 年，出獄後根本不知道怎麼在社會上生存。

the third degree

3 慣 **審問；盤問**

When Gina didn't come home Friday night, she got **the third degree** from her mom and dad the next day.

吉娜星期五晚上沒回家，隔天被爸媽盤問了一頓！

heat 可表「壓力」，而警察就是對你施加壓力的人，要你遵守法律，遵照指示，因此 **the heat** 是「警察」的別稱，源於北美。

the joint（監獄）源於北美，和之前介紹過的 the can、the slammer 可以互換使用。

被問一連串詳細的問題，就可用 get/give someone **the third degree**，通常是在警局被警察訊問，或被父母問話。

the man

1

名 警察；政府；白人機構；當權者

For a long time, African-Americans saw **the man** as the enemy. They felt that they were not there for their protection but to harm them and make their lives more miserable.

有好長一段時間，美國黑人都把美國政府視為敵人，他們覺得政府不但不保護還迫害他們，讓他們的生活更悲慘。

2

名 在某個領域表現傑出者

Anyone who has ever played basketball thinks that Michael Jordan is **the man**!

只要是打過籃球的人，都覺得麥可‧喬丹是天王！

3

名 做出偉大事蹟或很酷的人

Paul is **the man**. We went camping this weekend, and he did everything he possibly could to allow us to have the greatest time!

保羅是英雄！我們這週末去露營，他幾乎一手包辦所有事，讓我們玩得超開心！

4

名 毒販

Ken had to go see **the man** about getting some party favors for the weekend. There was a big rave and he wanted some pills.

阿肯要去找毒販弄點週末狂歡派對用的小禮物，他想帶點藥丸去。

the Man Upstairs

5 慣 上帝

Whenever you need someone to talk to, you can always talk to **the Man Upstairs**. He is always listening.

不論何時只要你想找人說說話，都可以找上帝，祂隨時都願意聆聽。

美國黑人把當權者稱為 **the man**，這個用法帶有貶義，自美國黑奴時期，有些黑人覺得只要是白人就跟有色人種過不去，覺得 the man（政府）是惡霸，讓他們過得很悲慘。

頂尖的運動員、巨星、藝術家在他們的圈子裡，也會被稱為 the man，就像天王、神人一樣，這可是很光榮的事。

完成偉大的事情也能讓你成為 the man（英雄），大多是家人或朋友才會這麼稱呼你，通常在開玩笑。

有些人認為自有時間以來，上帝（the Man）便一直存在，有人把上帝稱為 **the Man Upstairs**（樓上的人），而 upstairs 指的就是天堂，大多是信神者會這麼說。

上述這四個用法都相當常用，至於用 the man 表示「毒販」則只用於毒品圈，想要買毒品的人，都這麼稱呼毒販。

the real thing

1 慣 真實的人或事

So many people go through life trying to find **the real thing**. The question is what exactly is the real thing and how do you know when you found it?

很多人一生都在尋找人生真諦，問題是什麼才是真諦，你又怎麼知道你找到了？

the real McCoy [mə`kɔɪ]

2 慣 真品

The thief had a funny feeling that the painting he heisted wasn't **the real McCoy** but a copy of the original.

小偷隱約覺得他偷的那幅畫不是真跡而是贗品。

　　這兩個詞意義相當類似，不過 **real thing** 用得更頻繁，描述感覺、人或東西，最常在愛上某人或找到真愛時使用，例如：

When I met Peter, I just had this feeling that this was the real thing!

我一遇見彼得，就知道他是我的真命天子！

　　the real McCoy 的來源是美國曾經有個拳擊手，稱號叫 Kid McCoy，某天在酒吧裡，有人吹牛說：「他可以輕易打敗 Kid McCoy。」，結果 Kid McCoy 本尊聽到了，就把那個吹牛的人揍了一頓，因此 the real McCoy 引申出「真品」或「真人、本尊」之意。

the shitter

1 名 廁所

Tim hated to use **the shitter** at work because there wasn't much privacy.

提姆不喜歡在公司裡上廁所，因為那裡沒什麼隱私。

the runs/the shits

2 名 拉肚子

Eating beans makes some people get **the runs**.
有些人吃豆子就會狂瀉。

After eating Mexican food and drinking a lot of beer, Adam got **the shits**.
亞當吃了墨西哥菜，又喝了很多啤酒，結果落賽了。

　　the shits（拉肚子）源自英國，我們一看the shitter（廁所）就能了解那是什麼地方了。

　　這三個詞都是比較粗野的講法，多數人都不說甚至不想聽到，不過，就是有人喜歡講他們的腸胃活動，the runs和the shits（拉肚子）都不是很愉快的事，多數人都不想用這樣的用語描述在廁所裡的經歷。

thrash [θræʃ]

1 名 吵鬧、奢華的派對

There was a group of girls who were leaving Taiwan to go back home for good so we had a huge **thrash** to say our last goodbyes.

一群女生要永別台灣回家鄉，所以我們開了一個狂歡派對為她們餞行。

2 名 節奏快速的搖滾樂

Some people think **thrash** is great music to dance to, but I can never seem to find my groove with it.

有些人覺得 thrash 音樂很適合跳舞，但是我從來就不這樣覺得。

3 動 故意或是無法控制地亂衝亂撞

When Ryan doesn't get what he wants, he'll throw himself on the ground and **thrash** around. I always let him do this until he wears himself out.

雷恩如果得不到他想要的東西，就會在地上打滾，我每次都由他去，等他累了就會停了。

用 **thrash** 表示「吵鬧、奢華的派對」，這種用法源自英國，在美國不太常用。

thrash 又稱為 thrash metal（敲擊金屬），是一種重金屬搖滾樂，速度極快，它並不普及，大多數的舞廳、酒吧都不會演奏或播放這種音樂。聽 thrash metal 的人跳舞時，看起來就真的是在亂衝亂甩，把手和頭甩啊甩的。

throw up [ˈθro ˈʌp]

1 片動 嘔吐

Brenda was so nervous about giving a speech in front of hundreds of people that she **threw up** before going onstage.

布蘭達要在好幾百人面前演講，上台前緊張到吐。

throw a fit

2 慣 發飆或很驚訝

My mom **threw a fit** when she found out that Lewis and I got married.

我媽發飆了，因為她發現我跟路易斯結婚了。

throw a sickie

3 慣 裝病

At least once a month, she will **throw a sickie** and spend her day painting in the park.

她每個月至少會裝病一次，跑到公園裡畫一整天的畫。

throw up 最常用來表示「嘔吐」，讓你有第二次機會看看你剛剛吃進了什麼。

throw/have a fit 表示發生了什麼事，讓你「發飆」或是「很驚訝」。

throw a sickie 是個有趣的用語，就是藉口裝病，不去做應該做的事。

tongue bath

1 舔遍全身、濕濕的吻

Nina hates to watch movie scenes in which the actors are giving each other **tongue baths**.

妮娜最討厭看電影裡演員互相舔遍全身那種濕濕的吻。

tongue job

2 快速猛力的一吻

Monica kissed a boy named Mike McMann. He was the worst kisser ever. He gave **tongue jobs** instead of the soft passionate kisses that she preferred.

莫妮卡以前親過一個叫作麥克‧麥可曼的男孩，他的吻技真是世上最差的，他只會快快地用力一親，根本不會她喜歡的那種熱情柔軟的吻。

3 為女性口交

Some men enjoy giving **tongue jobs** when others would rather not do it at all.

有些男生還滿喜歡幫女生口交，但有些則敬而遠之。

tongue sushi

4 喇舌

A kiss shouldn't be described as **tongue sushi**. Sushi is a Japanese dish. How unromantic is that?

法式熱吻實在不該叫作「舌頭壽司」，壽司可是日本菜耶，真不浪漫啊！

tongue wrestle

5 慣 喇舌

Janice doesn't think **tongue wrestling** should be done in public. "If you want to be with someone who likes that, do it behind closed doors," she said.

珍妮絲覺得不該在公眾場合喇舌，她說：「如果你想跟喜歡幹這種事的人在一起，關起門再做吧。」

　　上述俚語都源於美國。接吻的方式有很多種，而接吻的說法也有很多種：

　　tongue bath 是用舌頭舔遍全身，像是用舌頭洗澡一樣。

　　tongue job 比較常出現的意思是「為女性口交」。

　　熱情的吻或喇舌除了 French kiss（法式熱吻），也可說 **tongue wrestle**（舌頭角力）或 **tongue sushi**（舌頭壽司）。

tool [tul]

1 名 陰莖

Men already have big enough egos. Why do they need to call their penises **tools**?

男人已經夠自負了，為什麼還要把陰莖叫作「神器」？

2 名 傻瓜

Mattie felt like the biggest **tool**. He spilt coffee all over himself during lunchtime.

馬帝覺得自己真是大白痴，他午餐時把咖啡潑得滿身都是。

3 名 槍或武器

The general told his men to grab their **tools** and ammunition and to get in the truck.

將軍命令手下拿好武器和彈藥，坐上卡車。

4 名 被人當作工具使的人、爪牙、傀儡

These knights think they have power, but they're just the king's **tools**.

這些騎士自以為握有權力，其實他們只不過是國王的爪牙。

tool along

5 片 動 悠閒自在地開車

He **tooled along** the freeway.

他在高速公路上悠閒地開著車。

tool around

片動 閒晃

When Andrea has nothing better to do on Sunday afternoons, she will **tool around** her neighborhood.

安卓雅星期天下午沒事做的時候，會在家附近亂晃。

　　tool 原意是「工具」，當俚語時和原意接近的用法是「槍」或「武器」，在軍警界會使用 tool 保護自己和週遭的人，因此槍和武器也算是一種工具。

　　如果有人犯傻，可用 tool 半開玩笑地說他是傻瓜，這樣的用法多用於朋友之間。

top banana

1

名 主要的負責人

Bethany thought that she was the **top banana**, and she always treated others as if she were better than them.

貝珊妮自以為是老大,每次都一副高人一等的樣子。

top dog

2

名 頭頭、老闆

Tom is the **top dog** at his company, but he treats all his employees fairly, and they respect him.

湯姆是公司老大,他對員工很公平,因此員工都很尊敬他。

 對很多人來說,當第一名是一件很重要的事,終其一生努力奮鬥就為了當上公司的總裁或主管,或成為該行業的領導人物(**top banana** 或 **top dog**),不過,「最頂尖的香蕉」或「最頂尖的狗」比較多用來開玩笑,不適合用於正式場合。

total ['totl]

1 ⑩ 殺死、毀滅

The typhoon **totaled** cities and towns all across Southeast Asia. Many people were killed in the storm.

颱風摧毀了東南亞各地的城市和鄉鎮，很多人在這場風暴中喪生。

2 ⑩ 完全受損

Keith took his friend's car and drove it while he was wasted and completely **totaled** it.

基斯跟朋友借車，酒駕把車撞得稀巴爛。

totally

3 ⑪ 表示同意

"Did you see the special effects in that movie? Weren't they the best you have ever seen?"

"**Totally**!"

「你有沒有看到那部電影的特效？是你看過最棒的吧？」

「那還用說！」

total 原意是「整個的、全部的」，因此用 total 表示「殺死、毀滅、損害」時，就表示人或物完全被毀壞無法修復了。媒體、軍隊中講到交通事故時，常常用到這個字。

total 近年來最常用的說法就屬 **totally**（對啊）了，八○年代，住在洛杉磯外圍的人創造了一種特別的語言，叫作 Valley Girl Lingo（谷地女孩語），這些人說話每說幾個字就會冒出一個 totally，後來傳遍了全美至今。

254

trash [træʃ]

1 ⟨動⟩ 蓄意攻擊某人或毀壞某物

At the concert, things got out of hand and a lot of the fans started to **trash** the place. They ended up causing thousands of dollars worth of damages.　演唱會場面失控，很多歌迷開始破壞場地，造成價值好幾千元的財物損失。

trashed

2 ⟨形⟩ 喝醉的

It was Liz's last day in town, so all her girlfriends took her out and got her **trashed**.　那是麗茲待在鎮上的最後一天，所以她所有女性朋友把她帶出去灌得爛醉。

white trash

3 ⟨名⟩ 窮苦白人

This area of town, with its trailer parks, is inhabited mainly by **white trash**.　城裡有拖車屋停車場的這帶大部分是窮苦白人住的。

　　多數人一聽到 trash，馬上會想到原意「垃圾」。當動詞是指「蓄意攻擊」，競選期間最常發生。trashed 當形容詞，源於美國，年輕人較常用，是指「喝醉的」。
　　white trash 指美國南方貧窮的白人，帶有貶義，用來攻擊別人或自嘲，這群人因貧窮，所以沒辦法受良好教育。

A
B
C
D
E
F
G
H
I
J
K
L
M
N
O
P
Q
R
S
T
U
W
Y
Z

tuck/tucker [tʌk]

1 名 食物

For the potluck dinner, everyone is bringing his or her favorite **tuck** and sharing it with everyone else.

百樂晚餐派對就是每個人帶一份自己最愛吃的菜跟大家分享。

Tim went to the 7-Eleven and grabbed a load of **tucker** because he had the late-night munchies.

提姆跑去小七買了一大堆食物,因為他一到了深夜就嘴饞。

tuck into

2 片 動 吃得津津有味

It's funny to watch Amanda order food and then **tuck into** it. She has a good appetite and always enjoys her meals.

每次看阿曼達點餐、吃得津津有味,總覺得很有趣。她胃口很好,吃什麼都好吃。

　　這三個俚語最常用的是 tuck into(吃得津津有味),tuck 的原意是「把東西塞進或藏在一個舒適、安全、隱密的地方」,和俚語用法有些相似,吃東西就是食物塞進嘴巴。

tuckered

1 形 疲倦的

Stella was **tuckered**. She couldn't keep her eyes open another second.

史黛拉累壞了，完全無法再把眼睛張開。

tuckered out

2 片 動 累壞的

After playing at the amusement park all day, Isabella and Grace were all **tuckered out** and fell asleep in the car on the way home.

伊莎貝拉和葛蕾絲在遊樂園玩了一整天都累壞了，回家時在車上睡著了。

tuckered 和 **tuckered out** 源於美國，主要用於美國和加拿大，兩者可替換使用。當你tuck someone in時，就表示你把他放到床上，為他蓋好被子，讓他好好睡覺。這也是tuckered (out)的來源，一個人疲倦或累壞時，只想要躺在床上裹在被子裡睡覺。

turn off

1 **名** 倒胃口的事物

Most women find men in tight swim shorts be a huge **turn off**.
很多女人都覺得男人穿緊身泳褲很噁心。

turn on

2 **名** 使人性興奮的事物

Olivia finds a kiss on the back of her neck or her shoulder blade to be a total **turn on**.
奧莉維亞覺得親她的脖子後面和肩胛骨都會讓她很興奮。

3 **片 動** 興奮、著迷

It is always exciting at the beginning of a relationship because you get to spend time discovering what **turns** your partner **on**.
戀愛初期總是令人興奮，因為你會花時間去找讓另一半興奮的方法。

　　要記住這幾個字的用法，最好的辦法就是想像自己身上有個開關，可以 turn on（打開），也可以 turn off（關掉）。噁心的人或東西會把你的開關關掉；有吸引力的人事物則會把你的開關打開。

　　通常說 turn on 指的是兩個人之間的感覺，像是一個微笑，可能就會讓人興奮或著迷，對方也會因此想要更了解你，當然外表也能挑起對方的性慾，身材、眼睛、嘴巴、衣著或舉止都可能讓人產生「性」趣，多在約會時說。

turn over

1 片動 （地方）被盜

Mr. and Mrs. Jones came home one night to find their house had been **turned over**, and most of their possessions had been stolen.　瓊斯夫婦有天晚上回家時發現家裡被闖空門，大部分的財物都被偷走了。

2 片動 突擊或搜查房宅

The police went back to the suspect's house, and after **turning** it **over** for an hour, they found enough evidence to send the man to prison.　警方回到嫌犯家徹底搜查一個小時，最後找到了足以送他入獄的證據了。

turn over a new leaf

3 慣 改過自新；重新開始

After Joe got caught cheating on his exams, he decided to **turn over a new leaf** and study hard to get results.

阿喬被抓到考試作弊以後決定改過自新，用功讀書，考得好成績。

turn over 源於英國，在英國相當常用，其中最常用的用法是「盜取」。

turn over a new leaf 常用於某人想要改掉舊習或惡習，重新出發時。

259

twig [twɪg]

1 名 曲棍球桿

The boys grabbed their **twigs** and hit the ice.

男生們抓起球棍，去打曲棍球了。

2 名 身材很瘦的人

The man walking on the beach looked like a **twig**. It seemed like he hadn't eaten in days.

走在海灘上的那個男的瘦得像根樹枝，看起來好幾天沒吃東西了。

　　加拿大的曲棍球迷會把「曲棍球桿」稱作 twig，曲棍球是加拿大最盛行的運動，但曲棍球在美國沒那麼風行，因此用 twig 表示「曲棍球桿」的用法也沒那麼普遍。

　　用 twig 形容「骨瘦如柴的人」，源於美國。twig 原意是「細小的樹枝」，用來形容人有兩種方式，你可以說某個人整個人就是很瘦，也可以說他身上某個部位很細瘦，例如：

He has twigs for legs.

他兩條腿好細。

140

under the table

1 〔慣〕 喝醉酒

After a few too many beers, Maggie was **under the table**.

多喝了幾杯啤酒後，瑪姬醉倒了。

2 〔慣〕 私下；檯面下

The liquor store was busted for selling alcohol to minors **under the table**.

酒店被抓到私下賣酒給未成年者了。

under the weather

3 〔慣〕 身體不舒服

Tracy has been a bit **under the weather** ever since she came back from her vacation. She doesn't know if she caught the flu or if she just misses traveling.

崔西旅行回來後身體一直不太好，她不知道自己是感冒，還是只是懷念旅行的日子。

　　under the table 最常用來表示「喝醉酒」，想像人喝多了酒，從椅子上滑到桌子下；非法交易也是偷偷進行，用 under the table 來形容。

　　under the weather 也很常用，用來描述「身體不舒服」。這兩個俚語都源於美國。

uptight [ˋʌpˋtaɪt]

1 形 精神緊張的；壓力很大的

Leann is so **uptight**. Ever since she agreed to work on this project she hasn't been herself.

琳恩真的壓力很大，自從她答應接這個案子以後就不太對勁。

2 形 古板的；保守的

Amelia needs to stop being so **uptight**. She should just learn to stop worrying about what others think of her and do what she really wants to do.

艾蜜麗雅不能再這麼ㄍㄧㄥ了，不該再擔心別人怎麼看她，做自己想做的事就好了。

up shit creek

3 慣 惹上大麻煩

The girls went camping and one of them forgot to bring the poles for the tent. They were **up shit creek**.

一群女生跑去露營，結果有人忘了帶帳篷架，這下麻煩大了。

up the creek

4

慣 麻煩大了

Troy was at the airport ticket counter when he realized he had left his passport in the taxi. He was **up the creek** because there was no way he'd be able to find the taxi that dropped him off.

卓伊到機場櫃檯報到才發現把護照忘在計程車上，麻煩大了，因為他根本沒辦法找到載他來的計程車。

drive someone up the wall

5

慣 發瘋、狂怒

Sarah is **driving me up the wall**. She can never do anything for herself, and she expects me to do everything for her.

莎拉真的快把我逼瘋了，她自己什麼都不做，只等我幫她做所有的事。

　　這些俚語都源於美國，非常普遍，成年人最常說這幾個詞。

　　一個人很 **uptight**，就表示他「很緊繃，壓力很大」或是「很ㄍㄧㄥ」，無法放鬆享受生活。

　　up shit creek 和 **up the creek** 可互換，只要有人陷入困境而且後果不堪設想時，就可用這兩個片語。

　　要記住 **drive someone up the wall** 的意思，就想像如果你被逼瘋了，想馬上翻牆逃離的情況。

U

wack

1 形 差的、爛的

Whose **wack** idea was it anyway to go hiking in this awful weather?

這麼糟的天氣來健行是誰的爛主意啊？

2 名 瘋子

Don't believe a word that **wack** says.

不要相信那瘋子說的話。

3 名 愚笨的想法；胡說八道

That speech she made was full of **wack**.

她的致詞根本就是胡說八道。

wacko [ˋwæko]

4 名 發瘋、精神錯亂的人

There was a woman in the restaurant wearing clothes from the 1800s. She was sitting at a table with two meals and yelling at some guy named Nathaniel that wasn't there. She was a complete **wacko**.

餐廳裡有個女的穿著 1800 年代的衣服坐在那裡，桌上有兩份餐，還對著一個叫作奈森尼爾的人大吼大叫，但那裡根本沒坐人，她真是瘋子。

wacky [ˈwækɪ]

5 形 古怪的

Daisy is **wacky**, and that's what I love about her. She wouldn't be the same person if she weren't always trying something new and different.

黛西真是古靈精怪，不過這也是我喜歡她的點，如果她不嘗試新奇的事物，就不是黛西了。

wacked

6 形 疲倦的；累壞的

The boys are always so **wacked** when they come back from the water park.

每次男孩們去水上樂園玩回來都累壞了。

　　wacko (whacko) 和 **wacky (whacky)** 是用來指瘋狂或古怪的人。**wacko** 指真正精神錯亂的人，多形容陌生人；而 **wacky** 則多半開玩笑地描述那些與眾不同，卻自得其樂的人，多是朋友和家人之間會說的話。

walk [wɔk]

1 動 獲得自由

The guard went up to the prisoner and told him he would be **walking** by the end of the day.

警衛走向囚犯跟他說，他那天傍晚就可以走人了。

2 動 消失；逃跑

In the movie, the main character **walks** and no one ever sees him again.

電影裡的男主角就這樣消失了，再也沒有人看過他。

walking papers

3 名 解雇通知

Bryan had been working at the company for six months when he was given his **walking papers**. His boss told him they needed to downsize, and he was here the least amount of time.

布萊恩在公司做了半年後收到解雇通知，他老闆跟他說要裁員，而他的年資最淺。

take a long walk off a short pier

4 慣 叫對方滾開

Blair was in a bad mood, so when a guy tried to chat with her at the bar, she told him to go **take a long walk off a short pier**.

布萊兒心情不好，在酒吧有個男的想搭訕她，她叫他滾去死。

> walk（走路）當俚語時，表示「重獲自由」和「消失」。拿到 **walking papers** 也算是另類的自由。
>
> **take a long walk off a short pier** 源於美國，比 get lost（滾開）還要不客氣。

264

wanker [ˈwæŋkɚ]

1 图 卑鄙小人

Sam is such a **wanker**. He is always making everyone else's life miserable.

山姆真是小人，老是讓大家不好過。

2 图 沉溺於自慰的人

If someone is a **wanker**, they masturbate a lot.

如果指某人是 wanker，就是說他常打手槍。

wankered

3 形 爛醉如泥的

Stella woke up the next morning to find 10 completely **wankered** people lying on her living room floor. They had been awake all night drinking beer.

史黛拉隔天早上醒來發現客廳裡躺了十個不醒人事的醉鬼，他們喝了一整晚啤酒。

　　wanker 和 **wankered** 都源自英國，每個英國人都知道，其他地方並不那麼普遍。

　　其中屬 wanker 最常用，通常都指男人，討人厭、沒禮貌，或做了傷害別人的事的「卑鄙小人」，都可被稱為 wanker。

wasted ['westɪd]

1 形 精疲力竭的

After finishing the triathlon, Carla was **wasted**. She went home right after the closing ceremony.

比完鐵人三項後卡拉真的累斃了,閉幕典禮一結束她就回家去了。

2 形 喝醉的

Allison hates going to the bar because guys who are **wasted** and smell like alcohol always hit her on.

艾莉森很討厭去酒吧,因為總會有喝醉酒、滿身酒味的男生跟她搭訕。

3 形 吸毒後變得嗨的

There were still people dancing at 9 AM at the beach party. The only reason they were still up was because they were **wasted**.

早上九點了還有人在海灘派對上跳舞,他們還這麼嗨的唯一原因就是吸了毒。

4 形 露出習慣性使用毒品之跡象的

Karen noticed that her friend James had all the tell-tale signs of someone who had become **wasted**.

凱倫在朋友詹姆斯身上發現所有染毒的人會有的徵兆。

　　waste 原意是「浪費」,也就是「用得過多」,這也是它的俚語用法所具有的涵義:熬夜熬太久、喝酒喝太多,或是吸毒吸太多。大學生和二十幾歲的成年人都很愛用 **wasted**,描述他們在短時間內喝太多酒、吸太多毒之後所處的狀態。這個用法源自美國。

whack [wæk]

1 **動** 雇用殺手謀殺人

The mob boss told Ralph the Razor to **whack** Joey Jr. because he ratted them out.

黑幫老大叫剃刀瑞夫把喬伊二世給幹掉，因為他出賣了他們。

2 **形** 怪怪的

Crystal is so **whack**. Her apartment is a good example of how crazy and unusual she is.

克莉斯朵真是怪咖，從住的公寓就可以看出她有多瘋、多怪了。

3 **形** 瘋狂的；令人難以置信的

"Did you see that wave he just rode in on?"

"Yeah, that was **whack**!"

「你有沒有看到他剛剛衝的那個浪？」「有啊，真令人難以置信！」

whacker [ˈwækɚ]

4 **名** 怪人

Gloria is a **whacker** and she has to have everything in a certain way. She can only buy certain foods and shop at certain stores.

葛洛莉亞是個怪人，做什麼都有一定的規矩，只買某些食物，只在特定的商店買東西。

whack原意是「重擊」，俚語用法與原意相似，因為如果有人用這種方式對付別人，很可能會打死人。whack最常用來表示「雇用殺手謀殺」，這種狀況多發生於犯罪集團內。

whacked

1 形 精疲力竭的

After a crazy weekend at a music festival and a three-hour scooter ride with bumper-to-bumper traffic, the group was **whacked** by the time they got home.

一群人在音樂節度過了瘋狂週末，然後又騎著摩托車在路上塞了三小時車，回到家都累翻了。

whacked-out

2 形 酗酒後或吸毒後恍恍惚惚的

Lewis was **whacked-out** the last time I saw him. I think he's become totally wasted.

上次我見到路易斯時他恍恍惚惚的，我看他吸毒吸太嗨了。

whack off

3 片 動 手淫、自慰

Jimmy **whacked off** before he went to bed.

吉米上床睡覺前打了手槍。

whacked 表示「精疲力竭的」，常用於英國。

whacked-out (wacked-out) 表示「酗酒後或吸毒後恍恍惚惚的」，用於美國。

whack off 原意是「把東西剁成塊」，當俚語時指男性「自慰」，是較粗俗的說法。

wig [wɪɡ]

1 動 責罵

Marnie **wigged** her roommate because she borrowed her brand new shoes and wore them in the rain.

瑪妮把室友罵了一頓，因為她室友把她的新鞋借走，下雨天穿出門。

wig out

2 片動 失去理智的；欣喜若狂的

Every once in a while it's fun to completely **wig out**, and just go and do something you normally wouldn't do!

偶爾瘋狂一下也是挺有趣的，儘管去做你平常不會做的事吧！

wigger

3 名 模仿黑人的白人，特別用來指白人饒舌歌手

A lot of people think the biggest **wigger** in rap history is Vanilla Ice.

很多人認為饒舌音樂史上，最成功的白人饒舌歌手是凡尼拉・艾斯。

wig 源自英國，英國和北美使用的頻率差不多，原意是「假髮」，當俚語指「責罵」，和原意有點關聯：如果你正在罵人，對方可能會氣得想拔光頭髮，那他可就需要一頂假髮了！

wig out 表示「失去理智」，源於美國，很興奮或很生氣都有可能失去理智。

wigger 是 white（白人）+ nigger（黑人）混合而來的，指「模仿黑人的白人」，用於美國，有貶義，小心使用。

wipe out [`waɪp `aʊt]

1 片動 摧毀；傾覆

The typhoons have **wiped out** some small towns and villages in the mountainous areas of the island.

幾場颱風摧毀了小島山區裡的幾個小鎮和村落。

2 片動 謀殺

The man went to jail for life because he had **wiped out** four people.

那男人因謀殺了四個人被判終生監禁。

wipeout [`waɪpˌaʊt]

3 名 失敗

Mark felt like a **wipeout** when he didn't make the varsity team.

馬克沒被選進校隊覺得很挫敗。

wiped out

4 形 精疲力竭的

After packing everything up and moving, Valerie was too **wiped out** to start decorating her new place.

瓦萊麗把所有東西都打包好搬完家後，已經累癱沒力去布置新家了。

5 形 喝醉酒的

Everyone was **wiped out** after the Halloween Party. They gave away free drinks to those with the best costumes.

萬聖節派對結束後每個人都醉倒了，因為打扮最炫的人喝酒免錢。

wipe the slate clean

6 慣 既往不咎

Ted cheated on Amy a few months ago, so they split up. Now, they want to **wipe the slate clean** and start over again.

幾個月前泰德背著艾咪偷吃，兩人分手，現在他們想要不計前嫌，重新開始。

wipe out 最常指徹底摧毀一個地方或建築物；如果你累到只想上床睡覺時，也可說你已經 wiped out 了。

wipe the slate clean 的來源為以前的人在小店買東西可以賒帳，店家會把客人專屬的帳記在石板上，等到還清欠款，就會擦掉，從頭再記帳。之後引申為把以往的過錯、不和或債務等一筆勾銷，重新出發。

wire [waɪr]

1 名 警告信號

Across the bottom of the TV screen was a **wire** indicating that there was a weather emergency in effect.

電視螢幕下端有個信號，顯示正在發布緊急氣象警報。

wired

2 形 壓力很大的；緊張的；焦慮的

Nancy always seems so **wired** around the holidays. She has so many things to do: decorate the house, buy and wrap presents, and make Christmas Eve dinner.

南西似乎一到假期壓力就很大，她有好多事情要做：布置家裡、買禮物、包禮物，還要做耶誕大餐。

3 形 受某物刺激後精神亢奮的

The junkie in the park was **wired**.

公園裡那個毒蟲吸了毒很亢奮。

wired up

4 形 遭竊聽的

The undercover agent was **wired up** when he spoke with the mob boss.

臥底警察跟幫派老大談話時被竊聽了。

pull wires

慣 運用私人關係達到目的

He had his mom **pull** some **wires** to get him a promotion.
他靠媽媽的關係才升職。

　　wire（竊聽器）多使用於軍警界和特勤單位，為了查案而用竊聽器蒐集資料。

　　要記住 **wired** 表示「緊張的、壓力很大的」，就想像你被電線（wire）電到，嚇一大跳就不再緊張。

　　wired 也可以形容「受到某物刺激，變得亢奮」，是英國俚語。

　　pull wires 或 pull strings 都可用來表示「靠關係達到目的」，就是牽線的意思。

wise [waɪz]

1 形 詳知內情的

The reason why she got the promotion was because she was **wise** to the ways of advertising. Her ideas were very up-to-date and that was what the marketing executives were looking for.

她會晉升是因為她深諳廣告之道，她的點子都很新穎，符合行銷主管想要的。

wiseass

2 名 自以為風趣或自作聰明的人

Jon was such a **wiseass**, and he wasn't the friendliest coworker. Being in a working environment with him all day was unpleasant.

阿鐘老是自作聰明，一點都不是個友善的同事，整天跟他待在同一個地方工作真不舒服。

wise up

3 片 動 覺醒；醒悟

After staying out late three nights in a row, Olga **wised up** and went to bed early. She had a good night sleep and felt really rested in the morning.

連續熬夜三天後，奧嘉突然覺悟了早早上床睡覺，她睡了一夜好覺，隔天早上真的覺得自己得到了充分的休息。

get wise to

4 片動 知道；明白；懂得

I've **gotten wise to** all your tricks. You won't be beating me in this game anymore.

我已經摸清你所有的技倆，這場遊戲你別想再打敗我了。

put someone wise

5 名 讓某人知情

As the newest team member, Rob should be **put wise** to the situation.

身為新隊員，羅伯應該要知道現在的情況。

wise 可指你知道某件事的內情。**wiseass** 源於美國，形容那些自以為幽默或自作聰明的人。**wise up** 表示「覺悟」，突然領悟該怎麼做時，可以這麼說。

work [wɜk]

1 動 欺騙；詐騙

Some professional gamblers go to Las Vegas to **work** the casinos. Sometimes they end up winning a lot of money.

有些職業賭徒會跑去拉斯維加斯賭場騙錢，有時候還真能贏走一大筆錢。

work over

2 片 動 攻擊；痛打

Diana was **worked over** on her way home late one evening. She ended up in the hospital's emergency room.

黛安娜有天晚上回家路上被攻擊，還被送進醫院急診。

　　work 表示「欺騙、詐騙」的俚語用法相當普遍，從事詐騙的人會用這個字，愛拍馬屁的人也可以看作是這種人，當他們出於個人利益去做某些事情時，他們就是在work其他人。

　　work over 是毫不留情地用力揍，通常是為了得到什麼東西，或者出於報復。

Y

273

yuck [jʌk]

1 嘆 表示反感、不快

Anytime Cindy starts to pick her nose in class, the kid who sits next to her would say "**Yuck**!" This always makes her stop immediately.

每次辛蒂在班上開始挖鼻孔，她隔壁同學就說：「好噁心！」這樣她就不敢挖了。

yucky [ˋjʌkɪ]

2 形 可怕的；令人作嘔的

Dean thinks the taste of fish is **yucky**. He doesn't think there is anything that could taste worse.

迪恩認為魚的味道很噁心，他覺得沒有什麼東西比魚腥味更噁心了。

yuck 是表示反感的感嘆語，也可以拼成 yuk，源於美國，通常是小孩子覺得噁心時候會說的話，挖鼻孔、跌在泥地上或是不小心吃進小蟲子都可以說 yuck。

yucky 是形容詞，大人很少會說，通常是小孩用語。源於美國，形容像是食物、蟲子和會弄髒身體的東西等很噁心。

Z

274

149

zap [zæp]

1 動 殺死；摧毀

The noise the skeeters make when they get **zapped** by the electric fly swatter is weird.

蚊子被電蚊拍電死的聲音實在好奇怪。

zapper [ˋzæpɚ]

2 名 遙控器

When Ben's friends are at his apartment, they always fight over the **zapper**. 每次阿班的朋友到他家聚會時，每個人都在搶遙控器。

zappy [ˋzæpɪ]

3 形 精力十足的

After their nap, the children tend to get **zappy**. The teacher can never get them to settle down.

小朋友睡完午覺後各個精力十足，老師再也搞不定他們了。

以上三個字都源於美國。**zap** 最常用來表示「殺死、毀滅」，而多數人最熟悉的用法，就是有人拿起電蚊拍把蚊子電死的時候。捕蚊燈就叫 bug zapper，蚊子被電的聲音跟 zap 的發音很像，就是這個聲音和動作使 zap 廣為使用。

zapper 也指遙控器，通常是指電視的遙控器。

275

150

zero [ˋzɪro]

1

名 沒用的人

Her husband is an absolute zero; she has to take care of everything for him.

她老公完全沒路用,她還得替他處理所有事。

zilch [zɪltʃ]

2

名 什麼都沒有;零

"Do you have any money I can borrow?"
"Nope. I have zilch."

「你有沒有錢可以借我?」
「沒,我半毛錢都沒有。」

zilch、zero、nada、nothing 都是「什麼都沒有」的意思,zero 形容人「不重要、沒價值」,就是很沒路用。

zilch 是一個非常受歡迎的片語,如果有人問你有沒有某樣東西或知不知道某件事,你可以用這句話代替 no,強調你什麼都沒有或你什麼都不知道。

zing [zɪŋ]

1 名 幹勁；熱情

Eating a good breakfast will give you **zing** for the rest of your day.

吃頓好早餐會讓你整天都充滿幹勁。

2 動 言語攻擊

The politician **zinged** his opponent in the debate.

政客在辯論中砲轟對手。

zingy [ˈzɪŋɪ]

3 形 愉快的；令人興奮的

The club had a **zingy** atmosphere on weekends.

酒吧週末時氣氛愉快，令人興奮。

zing up

4 片 動 使有生氣

Jessica wanted to **zing up** the place, so she painted all the rooms, added some framed photographs on the wall, and bought fresh flowers for the table.

潔西卡想讓整個地方看起來更有生氣，便把所有房間重新粉刷一遍，掛上幾張上框的照片，又買了鮮花擺在桌上。

這幾個字都源於美國，其中最常用的就是 **zing** 和 **zingy**，分別表示「精力」和「愉快、令人興奮的」。

Z

zinger　[ˈzɪŋɚ]

1 名 **令人驚訝、驚嚇之事或令人震驚的消息**

When Audrey told me she was moving to Italy to be with her boyfriend, it was a real zinger. I had no idea she was even thinking about it.

奧黛莉跟我說她要搬去義大利跟男朋友住的時候，我真的很驚訝，我根本就不知道她有這樣的想法。

2 名 **非常好的東西**

Sharon won the spelling bee! Her receiving this award was a real zinger!

莎朗贏了拼字比賽！她贏了這個比賽真是太讚了！

3 名 **有智慧的話、妙語**

At my wedding reception, my uncle made a few zingers during his speech that made everyone laugh.

在結婚喜宴上，舅舅在致詞時妙語如珠，把大家逗笑了。

zinger 的俚語用法都源於美國，最常用來表示「意想不到的事」，就像是突然被打了一巴掌或總統突然下台，在你意料之外，未必是好事，也未必是壞事，只是讓你變得更警惕。

zip [zɪp]

1 圏 發出咻咻聲的

When children play with their toy cars and airplanes, they often make a **zipping** sound to show how fast the cars and planes can move.

小孩子在玩玩具車和玩具飛機的時候，常發出「咻咻咻」的聲音，表示他們的汽車和飛機跑得有多快。

zip it

2 慣 閉嘴；安靜

When his students are talking and he is trying to teach, he would tell them to **zip it**! It is much nicer than saying shut up.

當他上課時學生講話，他就會叫他們安靜，這種說法比閉嘴委婉多了。

zip one's lip

3 慣 請對方閉嘴

Andrea, if you don't **zip your lip** now, I am not going to tell you what I found out from Mom the other day!

安卓亞，如果你不閉嘴，我就不跟你說我前幾天發現了媽媽什麼祕密！

叫某人 **zip it**（安靜），比 shut up（閉嘴）更委婉，老師或家長常常這樣跟孩子說，此時態度雖然很堅定，但不會太嚴厲。**zip your lip** 也是「閉嘴」，多用來命令較大的小孩或青少年，就好像是把嘴唇的拉鍊拉上，這兩個片語都源於美國。

zonk [zɑŋk]

1 動 打;擊

Andy has a bruise on his head because Bo zonked him during recess. 安迪頭上黑青,是下課的時候被阿波打的。

zonked

2 形 累壞的;疲倦的

They drove an hour, hiked to the campsite, set up the tent, and swam in the river all before the sunset. After dinner, they were all pretty zonked.

他們開了一個小時的車後,走路到營地,搭起帳棚,又趁日落前在河裡游泳,吃過晚飯後,他們各個都累垮了。

3 形 爛醉如泥的

Brian was zonked after a night of too many drinks.

布萊恩晚上喝了太多酒,結果醉到不醒人事。

zonk out

4 片動 睡死

He was so tired that he zonked out in the car.

他累到在車上睡死了。

　　zonk 原來是形容敲打東西時發出的聲音,多用於書面,少用於口語。zonked 形容累到不行。zonk out 表示「睡死」,叫不醒的程度。

俗辣英文俚語特搜（20K+1MP3）
Modern English Slang for You

作	者	LiLi Amanda Crum
譯	者	羅慕謙
審	訂	Helen Yeh
校	對	王鈺婷
編	輯	陳怡靜

內文設計排版	執筆者企業社
封 面 設 計	郭瀞暄
製 程 管 理	宋建文
出 版 者	寂天文化事業股份有限公司
電 話	+886-2-2365-9739
傳 真	+886-2-2365-9835
網 址	www.icosmos.com.tw
讀 者 服 務	onlineservice@icosmos.com.tw

Copyright 2014 by Cosmos Culture Ltd.
版權所有 請勿翻印

出版日期	2014 年 11 月	初版一刷
劃撥帳號	1998-6200	寂天文化事業股份有限公司

· 劃撥金額 600 元（含）以上者，郵資免費。
· 訂購金額 600 元以下者，請外加郵資 65 元。

〔若有破損，請寄回更換，謝謝。〕

國家圖書館出版品預行編目 (CIP) 資料

俗辣英文俚語特搜 / LiLi Amanda Crum 著；羅慕謙譯 .
-- 初版 . --
[臺北市]: 寂天文化 , 2014.11
　面；　公分
ISBN 978-986-318-292-4(20K 平裝附光碟片)

1. 英語 2. 俚語
805.123　　103019723